ADAM'S EMPORIUM

Ester Sharp once dreamed of becoming a doctor or dressmaker. But then her husband spent her small fortune and died young, leaving her penniless and pregnant. Now she lives in the slums, providing for her beloved daughter Polly by taking in mending and running errands. One such task is visiting Adam Boniface, the handsome pawnbroker, on behalf of her poor but proud neighbours. The two enjoy each other's company, and a warm relationship of mutual respect develops. But then a valuable gift sees Ester arrested on suspicion of theft . . .

We hope you enjoy this book.
Please return or renew it by the due date.
You can renew it at **www.norfolk.gov.uk/libraries**
or by using our free library app. Otherwise you can
phone **0344 800 8020** - please have your library
card and pin ready.
You can sign up for email reminders too.

SARAH SWATRIDGE

ADAM'S EMPORIUM

Complete and Unabridged

LINFORD
Leicester

First published in Great Britain in 2022 by
D.C. Thomson & Co. Ltd.
Dundee

First Linford Edition
published 2023
by arrangement with the author
and D.C. Thomson & Co. Ltd.
Dundee

A catalogue record for this book is available
from the British Library.

ISBN 978–1–4448–5116–8

A Shameful Errand

Ester Sharp carried her daughter in her arms as she pushed open the door to the pawnbroker's shop.

Mr Boniface stood behind the counter just as his father and grandfather had done.

It was gloomy, dark and dusty inside the shop and almost at once Polly began to wriggle.

'We won't be long,' Ester whispered as she kissed her little daughter's forehead.

There was something about the Emporium that Ester loved. It was like a museum packed with a mismatch of unusual objects, each with its own story to tell.

'Mrs Sharp,' Adam Boniface greeted her. 'What can I do for you today?'

He was a pleasant-looking man in his early forties. His face was kind and his eyes sparkled but there was a sadness there.

Perhaps he, like her, was widowed.

'I have these boots.'

Ester lifted a pair of dusty black ladies' boots on to the counter. They were still warm as her neighbour, Norah Bagwell, had only just slipped them off.

'I hope to reclaim them by the end of the week.'

Adam Boniface examined the boots to assess their value. She was aware he had watched her enter his premises wearing her own pair and could tell these did not belong to her.

They were far too big, for one thing, and besides, no-one in Charvil owned more than one pair of boots!

'I can give you six shillings,' he told her. 'You know the procedure. I'll keep them for two weeks in which time you may redeem them for six shillings and sixpence.

'After that time I reserve the right to sell them. Is that clear?'

'She knows — I mean, I know.'

They both knew Ester came to the pawnbroker on behalf of others. It was partly to protect their identity and hide

2

their shame, but also because she could read what he was writing down on the ticket.

Few of the local inhabitants were literate.

'Thank you, Mr Boniface.'

Polly, sitting on her hip, had spotted something she was interested in. Adam Boniface reached up and pulled down the toy rabbit that had caught her attention.

He bashed it against his leg a couple of times and a cloud of dust rose up, making him cough.

'Only sixpence to you,' he said, looking at Ester.

'I haven't any money to spare,' she said firmly. 'I know you mean well, Mr Boniface, but please don't tempt her with things she can't have.'

'I'm sorry,' he responded quickly. 'You're a good customer; take it as a gift for your loyalty.'

'I can't do that!' Ester was surprised. 'Thank you but I fear it would look like I'm profiting from my unfortunate neighbours.'

'I see.'

He smiled and Ester realised he must have been quite dashing in his youth.

'As you come in so regularly may I suggest we keep this toy to amuse your daughter while we conduct our business? Would that be acceptable to you?'

'That's very kind.' Ester smiled, grateful for his understanding. 'Does it have a name?'

Adam Boniface thought for a moment before answering.

'Herbert, after Mr Asquith.'

Ester suppressed a giggle; the rabbit bore no resemblance at all to the prime minister.

'Perhaps we should call him Bertie the bunny, then.'

'Bertie,' Polly echoed, giving the rag-rabbit a tight squeeze.

'That's right,' Ester told her. 'But Bertie lives here with Mr Boniface. You can see him again when we next come in.'

Ester picked up the pawnbroker ticket and nodded at Polly.

Solemnly the little girl handed over

the toy rabbit, then she gave Adam Boniface a huge smile.

'It looks like you've made a friend,' Ester told him, laughing.

She wasn't sure, but it certainly looked as though Mr Boniface blushed.

Extra Mouths to Feed

Ann Granger, Ester's neighbour, burst into Ester's one-roomed home.

'I've got work!' she cried. 'They want me up at the Manor House. They've got lots of guests staying and need some extra help.

'Some of the ladies haven't brought their own maids so I should get more money than usual!'

'And you want me to have Bobby and Mary?' Ester asked.

'I know it's not easy on you,' Ann apologised. 'But I'll give you half of what I earn, just like before.'

'You know I'll do it, Ann.' Ester laughed. 'I love having your two and we're not in a position to refuse any chance to earn a bit of cash.'

'You're right there!' Ann beamed. 'I must admit I can't wait to get back into my uniform. Mrs Walcot keeps it safe for me. She's good like that.'

'Well, you help her out, too, don't

forget. You're doing her a favour. It isn't easy to get a lady's maid at short notice.

'You know the house well and can slot in easily. I bet the guests won't know you're not part of the usual household.'

Ann nodded.

'I wouldn't be surprised if the family don't realise I'm not there on a regular basis any more, either. They probably think I just work below stairs. Well, except her Ladyship, of course.'

Ester swallowed the words she wanted to say, deciding they were best left unsaid.

It still made her cross that Ann had had to leave just because she was having a baby. Surely there were jobs she could have done until her baby was born?

Instead, she'd been dismissed just when she most needed a bit of money behind her.

'The sooner I can get there, the better,' Ann was telling her now.

The excitement in her voice was not lost on Ester, but then her neighbour loved being surrounded by all the beautiful things at the Manor House.

She'd be well fed, sleep on a proper mattress and not have to worry about where her next meal was coming from.

'Take what food there is in the cupboard. I don't know how long I'll be needed — it might only be a few days.

'If it's longer than a week I'll make sure I get some money to you. Is that all right with you?'

'I'll manage,' Ester reassured her friend, 'but I will empty your food store, thanks. I haven't enough to feed three children and myself.'

The women hugged and then Ester stood at her front door waving her off, with Bobby, Mary and Polly all standing close by.

★ ★ ★

Ann had been right; it wasn't easy being on your own. Ester now had extra mouths to feed.

Food was in short supply. Prices had gone up since the beginning of the war and so many men, like Ann's husband,

A Way Out

They hadn't been home long when there was a gentle knock on her door before it creaked open. There was never any privacy in Tinkers' Alley.

'Ester,' a grey-haired old man whispered. 'I need you to go and visit . . .'

He seemed to flinch when he caught sight of Bobby and Mary. Clearly he'd not expected her to have visitors.

'I need you to see Uncle.'

Many of the locals referred to Adam Boniface, the pawnbroker, as Uncle. They'd had the same name for his father and, no doubt, for his grandfather before.

No-one wanted to admit they didn't have enough money to last the week. Ester found this hard to believe as they were all in the same boat, but there were some very proud people around.

They would rather lie and tell elaborate tales about a rich uncle who had died and left them a small pot of gold. No-one took them seriously, but neither were they ever challenged.

'That's no problem,' Ester told him cheerfully. 'I can take something for you. How much do you need?'

The man removed his watch, looked at it one last time and handed it over.

'Rent's due,' he explained, 'and I'm already in arrears.'

'I'll do what I can,' she promised. 'I'll go first thing in the morning.'

That evening Ester prepared a broth made from what was left of Ann's vegetables and a few chicken bones.

Tomorrow she'd take the children and hunt for mushrooms in the fields that bordered the Manor House.

The soup was thin but hot and it warmed their insides. She set each child a task as she laid out their blankets beside the dying fire. The entire family shared the one room that was now Ester's home.

Bobby had to stack the firewood he'd collected earlier; Mary swept the floor and Polly picked up the shoes, one by one, and lined them up to the side of the fireplace.

Then they sat in front of the fireplace, huddled in their blankets as Ester told them a story.

'Tell us the one about the beautiful lady!' Mary begged.

'One day there was a lady just like your mother who had long, dark hair and big brown eyes.

'She was very pretty and she was clever, too. She lived in a huge manor house and was very happy . . .'

Ester continued with the story until Polly was curled up asleep next to Mary and Bobby's eyes were beginning to close.

Gently she kissed them all and covered them up to keep them warm.

The fire was nearly out, but she lit a candle which gave her just enough light to mend a garment which would bring in an extra shilling or two.

Ester sighed as she gazed at the three children sleeping peacefully.

She'd do anything to protect them but the thing she wanted most of all was to find a way for Polly and herself to leave the slums and return to a relatively easier life.

A life where she wasn't constantly eking out their meagre food rations or going hungry just so she could buy material for a warm coat to see Polly through the winter.

Ester wondered how long Ann would be away.

Although part of her wanted her friend to return soon it would be even better if Ann could earn a handsome sum to be shared between the two women.

More than anything she hoped Ann would return before Bobby and Mary began to worry that she wasn't ever coming back.

Feckless Husband

Nearly two weeks had gone by and there had been no news from Ann.

Ester understood that being in service meant that you were entirely in the hands of your employer. If they didn't grant you any time off, there was nothing you could do about it.

As the days went by Ester thought more and more about this. She'd known Ann for two years. It was Ann who'd helped her when she needed it most — the time had come for Ester to give birth.

The year 1915 had not been a good one for Ester. Her father had developed tuberculosis from one of his patients and just could not shift it. He'd died at the beginning of the year.

Her mother never came to terms with his loss and faded away, leaving Ester alone. She did, however, inherit her father's house and a tidy sum of money.

That was the time she had dreamed of following in her father's footsteps.

Unfortunately, coming into a small fortune had gone straight to her husband's head and he spent more than they had.

In no time at all he'd managed to accrue huge debts.

It was only when the house had to be sold that the solicitor spoke with Ester and she became aware of the dreadful situation she now found herself in.

Naïvely she asked her husband to talk with his creditors in order to buy time. She stood by her husband and promised him they'd both work together to pay back every penny.

Regrettably, the creditors were not willing to wait. The house had to be sold to pay them off and, when that took time, they beat him so severely that he died from his injuries. Not that anyone could prove anything.

Ester, as his wife, was liable for his debts. She lost everything.

The saving grace, in her eyes, was the fact she was left with the most precious gift of a child.

Not that Polly resembled her father at all. The child was like a miniature version of Ester right down to the coppery gold curls that framed her pale face.

Over the last two years, since Ester's husband's demise, she had helped many people. It was time to ask a few favours in return.

Ester arranged for a neighbour to mind the three children while she went to the Manor House to try to get word of Ann.

As she set out on her journey Ester passed by the pawnbroker's with its three golden orbs hanging outside.

On impulse she slipped inside and was pleased to see Mr Boniface sitting at his desk with no customer in sight.

'Mrs Sharp, what a pleasure.' He stood and gave her a little bow. 'No Polly today?'

'Good morning to you, sir,' she replied. 'I am on a mission today to find news of my good friend, Ann, who has been working at the Manor House for the past fortnight.

'I just wondered if you ever hear from anyone there?'

Adam Boniface shrugged.

'I gather they have been doing a great deal of entertaining, what with bringing in a good harvest and the celebrations that incurs.'

Ester had little knowledge of harvest festivals but this news made her feel better.

Perhaps Ann was being kept very busy and that was the reason she had not been able to send money.

'I am caring for her children and she promised to pay me but I haven't seen hide nor hair of her,' Ester explained.

She wasn't usually one for sharing her troubles with others, rather she was the one listening to other people's woes.

However there was something about Mr Boniface that she trusted and, once she'd started, she felt the need to share more.

'As I've told you before, Mrs Sharp,' Mr Boniface began, 'you bring me good business so I'm more than willing to help you out. I can lend you some . . .'

'No, no,' Ester responded quickly. 'I haven't come to you to ask for anything, although I am very grateful for the offer.

'I am more concerned for Ann. She must be working so hard. I'm sure she'd love to hear news of her children and they of her.'

The pawnbroker nodded.

'As it happens I often see Mrs Walcot, the housekeeper at the Manor House, at church on Sunday mornings.

'I shall make enquiries about your friend on your behalf. Would that help?'

'That would be very kind,' Ester replied. 'I am making my way over there now, just for my own peace of mind.'

'In that case may I escort you, at least part of the way? I have a delivery to make in that direction.'

'I would be glad of your company,' she said gratefully.

He collected up a parcel and turned the sign on the door to *Closed*.

Searching for Ann

Adam Boniface proved to be an interesting and entertaining walking companion. Having lived in the neighbourhood all his life, as had his family, he knew the area well.

He suggested they take a different route from the one Ester had originally intended.

'This path takes us along the river-bank and we'll come out near Whitecross Farm. It's a much quicker way to the manor.'

As they walked Ester confided how she came to be living in her current circumstances.

'I have to admit,' Mr Boniface told her, 'I am aware of your story.'

'You are?'

Ester was shocked. Other than Ann she had never told anyone.

'Did Ann tell you?'

'No, I do not believe I have met your friend. My information comes from my cousin.

'He's in the same line of business as myself and at least once a month we meet up and trade items.

'I am sure you can appreciate that some things sell better in the town while others are popular in the countryside.'

Ester nodded. She still didn't see how this had any bearing on her life story.

'As you are no doubt aware we have our regular customers, but occasionally unsavoury characters attempt to pawn stolen goods.

'Over the years one tends to get an inkling if someone isn't who they say they are.'

'I always thought you were a good judge of character, Mr Boniface,' Ester told him with a smile.

He returned her smile.

'Unfortunately my cousin was concerned when he received many visits from a Mr Sharp. He was clearly in some sort of trouble but the jewellery he pawned was of good quality.

'My cousin couldn't help but be suspicious. As part of his usual enquiries he asked if I knew the man.'

'And did you?'

Ester held her breath. She had always wondered what had happened to her mother's jewellery case. It had disappeared just after her father died.

At the time Ester had been worried about her mother's health and had never pursued its loss.

'I did. Mr Sharp had visited me on a number of occasions.

'We didn't always do business. Sometimes he felt I was not able to offer him enough and he chose to take his business elsewhere.'

Ester bowed her head in shame. Her husband could be the sweetest, most gentle man alive but at times he would show himself to be greedy.

'My cousin and I discussed Mr Sharp and looked into his background to make sure the items he was offering were actually his to trade.

'That's how we learned of your plight. Sadly your story is not unique.'

The pair walked in silence for a little

while. Ester was mulling over this information.

'He was a good man, really,' she said at last. 'Just weak when it came to business. He let others get the upper hand and soon got out of his depth.'

She was grateful Mr Boniface made no further comment. Instead he changed the subject and told her of the history of Whitecross Farm.

'If things had worked out differently in your life,' Adam ventured, 'I dare say you'd not be living in this neighbourhood?'

'No. From a young age I often helped Father with his patients. He taught me a great deal and I frequently thought about going into medicine when I grew up.'

'Do you still wish that now?'

That was one of the most likeable things about Mr Boniface, Ester decided. He treated her with respect and he took her seriously even when she was discussing her childhood dreams.

Once, when she'd been about ten,

she'd been at church with her parents and when they were leaving, the vicar asked a boy standing next to her what he was going to be when he grew up. The lad had no idea.

Ester told the vicar that she was going to be a doctor like her father. He actually laughed at her.

Her father had stood up for her.

'She'll make a fine doctor, too.'

She realised Adam Boniface was still waiting for her to reply.

'I'd still like to be a doctor, of course,' she said quietly, 'but I'm not in a position to go to university or medical school.

'Mother taught me how to sew and those practical skills are of more use to me now.'

'I'm sure they'll always be of use to you,' he said. 'Many a time I have tried to sew on a button but with little success.'

They were about to part company, with the Manor House just a stone's throw away, when they caught sight of Constable Harris and one of his men.

Constable Harris was older than Adam; in fact, he had retired a few years ago. Once the war started and men had signed up to fight for their country it was all hands on deck and Constable Harris once again had to don his uniform.

'Is everything in order?' Adam asked.

The constable looked at Ester. He seemed uncomfortable.

'We're just looking for something.'

Ester noticed what he was holding.

'That looks like Ann's coat!'

She reached out her hands to check it.

'Yes, this coat definitely belongs to Ann. I was the one who altered the pockets to make them deeper.'

'Ann?' Constable Harris asked.

'Ann Granger. She's been working up at the Manor,' Ester told him. 'She's all right, isn't she?'

'It's hard to say.'

He retrieved the coat.

'We found this in the ditch but there's no sign of its owner. It's a good quality coat, by all accounts.'

'She was given it by the mistress some

time ago,' Ester told him.

She didn't want Ann's good name to be questioned.

'I'm on my way to visit her.'

'I'll come with you to the Manor House, if I may?' Constable Harris said.

'I'll leave you,' Adam told her. 'Don't worry, I'm sure she'll be all right.'

Sadly, when Ester and Constable Harris visited the Manor House they learned that the house guests had all left the previous day.

Ann had been paid and had left the premises the evening before. She had been quite late leaving because she had stayed to eat with the staff.

Then Cook had insisted on sending her on her way with a basket of food for the children.

There was no sign of the basket. Nor of Ann or her wages.

Ester returned back home in a sombre mood but forced herself to put on a smile while she decided how to handle the situation.

In her mind there was no value in

worrying the children if Ann had simply found more work elsewhere.

She felt sure there was no point in mentioning the coat nor her friend's disappearance until they found out more details.

A Good Samaritan

A couple of days later Ester spotted Constable Harris in the market square. She caught his attention.

Neither of them spoke but the older man gave her the slightest shake of his head. Ester took this to mean there was no further news.

She left the market with the three children and headed up to the common. Up there, she knew, she would find an abundance of blackberries which would help fill their empty stomachs.

While they were there Ester considered the hazel trees which lined the edge of the field.

In a few weeks' time there would be nuts to eat — if the squirrels didn't get to them first.

Furthermore, early in the morning, when the mist was still on the ground, was the best time to find edible mushrooms.

Ester thought back to happier days

when she would go out early with her mother to pick them.

For lunch they would feast on a thick and tasty mushroom soup with fresh bread warm from the baker's oven.

She and the children returned home a couple of hours later, having eaten a meal of blackberries.

In her basket she had collected some windfall apples and a few wild plums. Could she make this food last more than one day?

Imagine her surprise when, on their return, she found a small box placed just inside her door.

At first she thought it must have been left there in error but her name was clearly written on the top.

It must have only just been set down. In this neighbourhood, if it wasn't screwed down the chances were that it would be stolen.

'What's inside?' Mary and the other two asked excitedly.

'Oh, my goodness!'

Ester raised her eyes toward heaven.

'Some good Samaritan has given us potatoes, a cabbage and a cauliflower. There are even a few carrots!

'We're going to eat well for the rest of the week.'

'And by then Mummy will be home,' Mary said hopefully.

'And maybe Daddy?' Bobby added.

'Don't be silly,' Mary told him. 'The war's not over.

'Daddy won't be coming home until the job's been done. He told us that, remember?'

Ester busied herself lighting the fire while the children fetched their blankets and huddled together on the stone floor until the logs started to burn and they began to feel some warmth.

Mary loved to sing, just like her mother, so she entertained Bobby and Polly for a little while.

This gave Ester time to hem a dress which could then be returned the following day for much-needed payment.

With only half an eye on the children Ester wondered if Constable Harris would try to contact Ann's husband to tell him she had gone missing.

As she finished her work she decided that, by the time the constable had written to Ann's husband, she would likely have returned and they would have troubled him unnecessarily.

Besides, he had a war to fight, so he had problems of his own.

Mystery Benefactor

Another week went by with no word from Ann. Without the occasional box of food Ester and the children would have all gone hungry.

She hadn't yet discovered who was leaving the life-saving provisions. It had crossed her mind that it might be the vicar, but he would have to treat all his parishioners the same, surely.

She knew for a fact that not everyone was as fortunate as she.

Eventually Ester came to the conclusion that perhaps her father had helped someone, in his capacity as doctor, and that this was the way his former patient was paying him back.

Nonetheless, she would have liked to know who it was so she could thank them in person.

On Friday Ester took the children into the pawnbroker's shop as she had a few errands to do.

Firstly she presented a ticket and

carefully counted out a number of coins to reclaim a pair of boots for a neighbour.

Then she handed over a pocket-knife from one of the market traders who was owed money by the innkeeper.

He, in turn, was owed money by the brewery. The problem was that the market trader still had to feed his family and pay his rent.

'Look at this!' Bobby cried as he pointed to a suit of armour hanging up in the corner of the shop. 'Does Daddy have to wear that?'

Ester smiled.

'No, Bobby, I think your daddy will have a much warmer and far more practical uniform.

'I'm sure he'll show it to you one day, when he comes home.'

Both Bobby and Mary always loved coming into the pawnbroker's shop.

It was full of weird and wonderful things. There were hats with enormous feathers poking out the top.

There was a stuffed baby crocodile

with sharp teeth and a dozen painted chamberpots.

Polly, too, looked forward to her visits and immediately sought out Bertie the bunny rabbit.

'He's been hoping you'd call in to say hello,' Adam Boniface told her in a quiet voice.

'Hello, Bertie,' Polly said.

She was talking a lot more, Ester had noticed, now that Bobby and Mary were living with them.

'Has there been any news?' Ester whispered to Adam Boniface.

Their eyes met and she knew she didn't have to go into any details.

'No good news, but then nothing bad, either. Remember that.'

Ester picked up the pair of boots to give back to her neighbour and the coins for the market trader, given in return for his pocket-knife.

She called to the children, gave Adam Boniface a little smile and glanced over at his desk.

It was at that moment that Ester

spotted a box which seemed not dis-similar to the ones she occasionally found on her doorstep.

She recalled the way her name had been written on the top and, looking down at the ticket for the knife, she real-ised she'd found her mystery benefactor.

But how on earth could she possibly thank him?

Hard Times

The following day Constable Harris called at Ester's home. When she saw who was at the door and greeted him he raised his hat and handed over Ann's coat to her.

'You may as well have this,' he told her simply.

Ester looked up at the policeman, searching his cold, grey eyes for more information.

Did this mean the police had given up any hope of finding her?

'Any news?' she asked him, speaking as cheerfully as she could so as not to upset the children.

'Nothing at all,' he replied. 'It is a complete mystery. Good day to you, Mrs Sharp.'

After he had left Ester hugged the coat to her chest.

Ann had been so thrilled when she'd been presented with it, she recalled, and the warm coat had served her well.

She would never have abandoned it. A good winter coat was a valuable asset.

As much as Ester would like to have kept the coat she knew she had no choice but to take it to Mr Boniface. She'd exchange it for whatever he could give her in return.

Times were hard and the price of everything had increased. It was becoming more difficult to feed both her and the children so any money she could raise from the coat would be a great help.

Then, of course, when Ann did return with her wages, she could always visit Adam Boniface — or ask Ester to do so on her behalf — and retrieve the coat.

When she next visited the Emporium with her bundle Ester came away suspecting that Adam Boniface gave her more than the coat was worth, but she couldn't bring herself to argue.

She had to feed the children.

She managed to eke out the money as long as she could but then Bobby had a growth spurt.

He had outgrown his britches and his

boots let in the rain, his shirt was patched in several places and he really needed a warm jumper.

Once again Ester counted the coins and tried to work out how she could get the best value for money.

Things were getting harder and harder for them all.

A Dreadful Decision

By Friday there was no food in the larder and only tuppence in the tin.

Ester's heart was breaking.

She had known this day had to come and now she couldn't put it off any longer.

Today, sadly, was to be the day she would hand Bobby and Mary over to the workhouse.

It was a dreadful decision to have to make but, without Ann's money, Ester couldn't feed them any more.

Dreadful though the workhouse was, at least there the brother and sister wouldn't starve.

The little group walked along slowly. Bobby kept stopping to pick up a conker or an interesting stone.

Ester wondered if the boy guessed where they were going.

Just as the dark grey stone of the workhouse building came into sight and Ester's eyes began to fill with tears she made out a lone figure walking toward them.

'Is that — ?' Bobby began.

'It's Daddy!' Mary shouted as she tore off down the road to greet the man.

As they drew closer Ester noticed the way her neighbour's husband now dragged his leg.

She also saw the pain around his eyes as he winced every now and again, but to his credit he didn't complain.

He hugged his children as he listened to Ester's story and thanked her over and over for taking good care of them.

They walked slowly back to the village with Mary skipping all the way. Even Bobby had a bounce back in his step.

'You should probably go to talk to Constable Harris. He may be willing to tell you more than he's said to me,' she told their father.

'Ann was last seen at the Manor House when the guests left, but then she disappeared. All that was found was her coat.

'I had to pawn it, I'm afraid, to feed the children, but I've kept the ticket safe for you.'

'You've done a great job,' Leonard Granger told her again. 'I can't thank you enough.

'But I'm here now and I've got a few bob on me. We'll be fine.'

Leonard smiled down at his two excited children.

'First thing tomorrow I'm going to see if I can find work somewhere. Even with this gammy leg there must be something I can do.

'Everything will be good from now on, you'll see.'

'Well, welcome home, anyway,' Ester said.

She could feel her shoulders relax a little. She was so relieved that she hadn't got as far as the workhouse and handed over the children.

'Here,' he told her, 'take this.'

He pressed a small, golden locket into Ester's hand.

'I got it for Ann, but, well, I want you to take it as a thank you. We must be in your debt.'

Ester's first instinct was to refuse such a valuable gift but now was not the time to be polite.

She still had Polly to feed, something that was always harder in winter when there was less food to forage from the hedgerows.

That evening the room seemed quiet without Bobby and Mary. Polly was curled up in a blanket sleeping peacefully.

This was always the loneliest time of the day for Ester.

She examined the locket. It was a pretty item of jewellery.

Under different circumstances she would have loved to have worn it.

Now, however, she knew she had no choice but to pawn it. Her only concern was how much she might get for it.

★ ★ ★

'What a very pretty piece,' Adam Boniface remarked as he peered at the locket and assessed its value.

'I imagine it was from a poor soldier who'd bought it for his loved one.'

'That's what I thought, and it seems Mr Granger had brought it back for Ann.'

'How is he?' Adam asked.

'He has injured his leg but he still seems fairly able and told me he was hopeful of getting work.

'In fact, it was his opinion that Bobby looked older than his years and that maybe he'd get some work, too.'

She left the pawnbroker's shop with what felt like a small fortune.

However, she knew that, by the time she had bought a little food and paid her rent, there would be precious little left of her bounty.

Accused

A day later there was again a loud knock on Ester's door. It was pushed open, letting in cold air.

Ester looked up from her mending and was surprised to see Constable Harris standing in her kitchen area once again.

'Have you found her?' she begged, jumping up and putting down her sewing. 'Is Ann OK?'

'That's not what I've come about,' Constable Harris told her.

His voice was as chilly as the winter wind.

'What is it, then?'

'I understand you pawned a gold locket recently,' he said.

'I did.'

'Can you tell me how you came to be in possession of such a valuable item of jewellery?'

Ester felt her heart beat faster. She wasn't sure where this conversation was going but it didn't feel right.

'I was given it as a thank you,' she told him.

She felt a loyalty to Leonard Granger because he was Ann's husband. It was only now she began to wonder how he'd actually come by the piece of jewellery.

'I need you to tell me who gave it to you,' Constable Harris continued.

'I don't think I'm at liberty to say,' she replied, her voice just above a whisper.

'Maybe it will help you remember if I tell you it was stolen some time ago and Lady Greenway wants the culprit punished.

'The loss of her property has caused her many sleepless nights.'

'Stolen!' Ester repeated. 'I thought it was from a soldier who'd died in battle.'

'Are you ready now to tell me the whole story?' Constable Harris gave a little smile but his eyes remained cold and hard.

'I can't say!' Ester pleaded.

She tried not to look at Polly who was playing with some scraps of material, waving them in the air like a flag.

'I don't want to have to repeat myself,' Harris said, his voice firmer now. 'The locket is stolen property. You took it to Mr Boniface where you pawned it and received money in return, is that not so?'

'I did pawn it but I didn't know it was stolen!' Ester's voice had risen a little as she started to panic.

'Mrs Sharp, I need to know who gave you the locket otherwise I will arrest you!'

Adam's Promise

Ester shivered in the cold damp cell. She fretted over Polly, wondering where her daughter had been taken.

Everything had happened so quickly! One minute she and Constable Harris had been merely discussing the golden locket, the next minute she was being carted off to a prison cell.

Nonetheless, Ester knew how things worked in this part of town. Nothing went on in private.

By now everyone would know of her arrest and someone was sure to come to her aid. Ann's husband would admit he'd given her the locket and she would be released.

The only problem could be if Leonard Granger had already found employment elsewhere and hadn't yet learned of her predicament.

No doubt it would only be a matter of time before word reached him and he would come and explain everything.

Ester thought of all those people she had helped over the last couple of years. She had never asked for anything in return.

Surely someone would step forward to help her! Everyone pulled together and helped each other in this area.

That was how it worked — or was it? Did they really accept her as one of them or had she always been considered an outsider?

'You have a visitor,' one of Constable Harris's men told her.

To her delight and relief Adam Boniface appeared at the door of her cell. He was so tall that he had to stoop.

'You have five minutes, no longer,' the policeman told him.

'I didn't tell him about the locket,' Adam assured her quickly. 'Constable Harris often comes into the shop and has a good look around.

'He spotted it straight away and started asking questions. I was as vague as I could be but, when he demanded to see the ticket, I had no choice but to hand it over to him.'

'I understand,' Ester assured him, 'but surely Mr Granger can explain.'

'That's what I am hoping, too,' Adam replied. 'I have a plan to help you, but I just wanted to let you know about Polly.

'She stayed with your next-door neighbour last night but the woman can't keep her any longer.

'I propose that I take her to my cousin's house. His wife will care for her until you're set free.

'They have no children of their own but I can vouch that she is a good and kind woman.

'Polly will be well cared for, I promise you.'

At the mention of her daughter's name Ester broke down. Tears trickled down her face.

Adam Boniface clearly was not the manner of man to stand by and watch a lady weeping.

He reached out and tried to comfort her as best he could.

'Time's up,' the guard told them.

'Don't lose faith,' Adam said as he was ushered out the door.

Once again Ester was left alone in the cold dark cell.

At least now, though, she could take comfort in the fact that Polly would be all right.

Mr Boniface had promised her and Mr Boniface was their friend.

Playing Detective

Adam was a bachelor in his early forties. He was considered too old for conscription and had lived alone ever since his father had died.

He had never had any experience of dealing with children but he'd grown fond of little Polly with her coppery curls and winning smile.

'Bertie!' she uttered excitedly on seeing him when he went to fetch her from the lady who'd been, reluctantly, looking after her.

'We'll go and fetch him now,' Adam promised her as he reached out for her hand.

'Excuse me!' the neighbour had also reached out her hand. 'I didn't have to take her.'

Adam threw a few coins in her palm and hurried away with Polly.

He was angry as he was aware of the kindness Ester had always shown this woman. It would sadden Ester to know her compassion had not been returned.

Adam and Polly collected Bertie the bunny rabbit then took a carriage to Adam's cousin's house, a short distance away.

Polly had never ridden in a carriage and laughed every time they went over a bump in the uneven road.

Once Adam had settled Polly with his cousin's wife he returned and began his search for Leonard Granger.

At first he was met with blank faces. It was as though no-one had ever heard of him.

Once he explained that Ester Sharp was being imprisoned because of him, however, he began to get some answers.

It seemed Granger and Bobby had become woodcutters and they slept in the forest. No-one knew what had become of Mary. Had the girl disappeared, just like her mother?

Adam knew he had no hope of finding Granger at night in the forest, but he discovered that the man would be paid on Friday for his logs.

There was a good chance the man would stick around for a pint or two at the King's Head.

Adam hated the thought of Ester spending another night in the cells, separated from her daughter, but there was nothing he could do.

The following day, however, he was up early. He headed down the path by the river that led to Whitecross Farm, just as he had the day he'd walked with Ester.

Adam searched the hedgerows where Ann's coat had been found. He was looking for clues as to what might have happened to her.

Sadly he found nothing.

In despair he visited the Manor House and spoke with Mrs Walcot, the housekeeper. She had not heard from Ann and was beginning to think the worst.

Before returning home Adam called in at the workhouse. There he was relieved to find Mary Granger.

At least that was one mystery solved and, although it was not an ideal situation, the girl was being fed and had a roof over her head.

He did ask the officials if they knew anything of Ann Granger but they had no record of her at the workhouse.

* * *

Friday couldn't come around soon enough for Adam. As the church bell struck five he shut up shop and headed toward the King's Head.

As luck would have it he spotted Bobby with his father and he approached him, trying to remain calm and controlled.

'Are you aware that the locket you gave Ester Sharp was stolen property? Now the police think she stole it and are treating her as a thief!'

'I don't know what you're talking about,' Leonard said as he turned and headed for the King's Head. 'Wait here for me, Bobby.'

He went inside the public house, slamming the door in Adam's face.

On seeing Bobby's expression, Adam knew the truth. The boy looked aghast at his father's reaction and lies.

Adam saw no point in punishing Bobby for his father's sins.

'Shall we go and find out who sells the best pies?' Adam suggested to the lad, whose eyes lit up at the thought of a tasty meat pie.

After having eaten one of the best pies in town Adam and Bobby headed back to the King's Head.

The noise coming from inside the inn was becoming more raucous even though it was still early in the evening.

'You'd better wait here, as your father told you to,' Adam instructed Bobby. 'I'll go and see if he's all right.'

The King's Head

As soon as he entered the inn Adam spotted Leonard Granger. He was leaning on the bar with a pint in one hand.

Adam stood in a dark corner for a while and watched. It was clear Granger had already drunk a few pints.

'Good evening, sir.'

It was one of Adam's customers. A pedlar, he often bought up trinkets that had been pawned to sell from his push cart as he wandered around from town to town.

'Hello, Mr Barnaby. May I buy you a pint?'

Adam didn't usually frequent ale houses but a plan was forming in his head.

'That would be mighty kind of you, sir.'

Adam made his way to the bar and purchased two pints of beer.

'We don't often see you in here,' Mr Barnaby said when he returned.

Adam explained Ester's plight and saw how Mr Barnaby reacted.

'That's not right! Ester Sharp's a good woman — an honest one, too. What's more, she'd never do anything that would endanger that little girl of hers!'

Mr Barnaby rose and headed to the bar.

Adam wondered if he was about to buy more ale. Instead, the pedlar approached Leonard.

'I was sorry to hear about your wife. I hear they haven't found her. Just as well Mrs Sharp took in your two children.

'She cared for them as if they were her own. It's not as though she's got any cash to spare herself.'

'I know that.' Granger waved his arm about. 'I thanked her.'

He swigged his beer.

'In fact, I gave her a golden locket. I'd got it for the missus but, as she wasn't around, I thought it would do for Ester.

'She ought to be grateful.'

Both men had been quenching their thirst for a while and their voices were growing louder with each pint.

Everyone at the bar had heard the conversation, including Constable Harris. Officially he was off duty but, in reality, he was never off-duty.

'Tell me more about that locket, Granger. Where did you get it from?'

'Found it,' Mr Granger slurred.

Constable Harris escorted him to the police station so he could sober up and remember in more detail.

Set Free

Ester was set free early the following morning. She wasted no time in hurrying home, longing to hold Polly in her outstretched arms.

The room was empty, of course, so Ester continued on to the pawnbroker's shop. Adam would know where she was.

As usual Adam Boniface sat at his desk behind the counter. The first thing Ester noticed was that Bertie the rabbit had gone missing.

'Where is Polly?' Ester asked urgently.

'With my cousin and his wife. I'm sure she's fine. As it's Thursday I close half day so I can take you over there to collect her.'

'Thank you so much!'

Ester reached out a hand, not knowing whether she was going to take his hand in hers or shake it.

'I felt so guilty because I had the locket on display and Constable Harris spotted it. I had no idea it was stolen, of course.'

'Neither had I,' Ester assured him.

'Thank goodness they let you go,' Adam said. 'I imagine Granger has given his statement?'

'I heard him say he'd found it but he was seen by a couple of people leaving Lady Greenway's property. In fact, the gardener had been chasing him off with a pitchfork!'

'No-one knew he'd stolen her jewellery.'

'Well, at least you're free,' Adam said.

She wrung her hands.

'He tried to imply that we were in it together — that it was my idea that he should steal from her while I distracted the groundsman!'

'He did what?' Adam stood up, his face flushed red with anger.

'Fortunately, a couple of people had been in to see Constable Harris. They told him how I'd been looking after Ann's children while she worked up at the Manor House, and how I'd continued to care for them even when Ann didn't return.'

'I'm glad you're free. I hated the thought of you being shut up in that cell and not being able to be with Polly. Don't worry, you'll be reunited this afternoon.'

'Thank you, Mr Boniface. Thank you so much!' Ester looked down at her dusty old boots. 'I don't know how I'm ever going to repay you.'

'You can start by calling me Adam.' He smiled. 'And may I call you Ester?'

A Business Proposition

As Adam and Ester rode in the covered carriage on the way to fetch Polly that afternoon Ester told him she'd had an idea.

'Your shop is full of goods. Some of those things have been in your shop for years; generations, even. Is that not true?'

He nodded.

'Well, yes, some things. That suit of armour, for example, has been hanging there since I was a child!'

She smiled.

'Exactly, and surely that's not good for your business. You need to sell what you have in your shop.

'At the moment too many things are just sitting there, collecting dust.'

'What do you propose that will change that?' Adam asked with a twinkle in his eye.

'I am thinking about some of the clothing you have on a clothes rack — because that's what I know about,' she explained. 'What if I took a few unsold items and added a ribbon here, a petticoat there? Maybe include a belt or change a neck-line?'

Adam shrugged.

'I know little about fashion. You're welcome to take what you want and do as you will.

'I have no idea whether your idea will work and they'll sell, but we won't know until we try.'

Adam smiled.

'I can either pay you by the hour and reimburse you for any materials, or you can have a percentage of any sales. Think about it.'

She considered.

'As we're both taking a risk I think it's fairer if I take a percentage. Then, if my idea doesn't work, you won't lose out.'

'But you will,' Adam pointed out. 'Why don't you choose, say, five outfits and work on them, noting the time you spend and the cost of any materials?

'Together we'll agree a selling price. We can display them in the window and take it from there.

'If they don't sell I'll have paid you for your time and reimbursed you. In turn I'll have modernised outfits which potentially have a better chance of selling.

'But if they do sell we'll split the profit 50-50. How about that?'

'I think that's very generous,' she assured him.

'Not in the least,' Adam argued. 'It is you who will be doing the work and it was your idea in the first place.'

'In that case, I accept,' Ester said with a smile. 'I confess I have my eye on a couple of dresses already.'

'I thought you might.' Adam smiled again. 'Does this make us business partners?'

'I suppose it does,' she agreed, 'but let's not get too hasty. The garments may spend the next five years collecting dust in your shop!'

★ ★ ★

Ester was so delighted to be reunited with Polly again that for a while she forgot about her business arrangement with Adam.

Polly had taken Bertie the bunny with her on her adventure. She didn't seem any the worse for having been separated from her mother.

Adam's cousin, Robert, and his wife had been kindness itself. Polly had been well fed and wore a new outfit courtesy of Robert and his own pawnbroker's shop.

Ester thanked them several times as she and Adam took their leave with the child.

The carriage set them down at the pawnbroker's shop and Adam led them inside.

Ester examined the clothing which hung on a rail made from a broom handle supported between two racks of shelves.

It reminded her of her father's study. It had had similar shelving but his had been full of medical books.

'Is this of any use?'

Adam held a small workbasket in his hands. The basket was round with an ill-fitting lid.

Bits of lace and lengths of ribbon tumbled out like ringlets.

'Your shop is full of treasures!' Ester gasped as she switched her attention from the dresses to the haberdashery basket.

'Actually, this was my mother's.' Ester heard his voice catch. 'It has been sitting by her chair ever since we lost her. I'd forgotten it was there.

'Please, take it. I have no use for it and she would be delighted to know it was being used.'

'That's very generous of you,' Ester said. She looked up into his eyes. 'I'll only accept it because we're business partners.'

He nodded, understanding her pride.

Polly was sitting on the floor. Adam had given her a cardboard box and a small blanket in which she'd wrapped Bertie. She was telling the toy rabbit a story before settling him down in the box to sleep.

'I've chosen five items as you suggested.' Ester held them out to show Adam.

Each item had a ticket pinned to the shoulder. It gave the date and the amount for which it had been originally pawned.

The only snag was making out Mr Boniface Senior's handwriting.

One was a nightdress so thin Ester could see her hand through it.

'What on earth are you going to do with that?' Adam exclaimed.

It was clear he thought it beyond repair.

'The lacework at the collar is beautiful,' she pointed out. 'I'm hoping to transfer it to this dress and use the lace from the hem to make matching cuffs. What do you think?'

He shook his head.

'I think it'll be nothing short of a miracle if you can sell any of these items. I do hope you're not going to be wasting your time.'

'On the contrary, when we were riding in the carriage to fetch Polly I was observing some of the ladies we passed. I believe I can bring these up to date.'

Her face lit up.

'In fact, I'm really looking forward to trying. It's so much more interesting than mending, trust me!'

A Favour to Ask

Adam called on Ester at her one small room on the ground floor. Other families lived above her and also in the basement.

Even on the sunniest day the room was never really filled with light, nor did it get any warmth except from the fire.

If Adam noticed these things he said nothing. Instead, he took Bertie out of his pocket and told Polly he'd come to visit.

'Are you checking up on me?' Ester asked playfully.

She held up what had been a plain brown dress. She had sewn the lace collar from the ancient nightdress on to the dress which instantly made it all the more interesting.

The lace cuffs, made from the hem, now gave the dress an air of sophistication.

'I'm impressed,' he told her.

Ester held up another dress.

'The hem was torn so I've shortened

it a little and I added these buttons for decoration. They were in your mother's basket and they're the perfect colour.'

Adam nodded his approval again.

'If you haven't come to see how busy I've been then what can I do for you?'

'I have come to ask you a favour. I have an important errand to run on Wednesday.

'It being half day closing for many it is often one of my busiest days. I wondered if you would care to mind the shop for me?'

Adam smiled.

'You can, of course, bring Polly with you and I have a good lamp on my desk by which you can sew. That's if you're not inundated with customers.'

'I'm willing to help you, certainly,' Ester replied, surprised. 'But I am not sure I am a good judge of the value of things.'

Adam laughed loudly, making Polly look up from where she played with Bertie.

'In the last few weeks you have brought

me, among other things, a pocket watch and a rug. Whether you were aware of it or not I was training you, telling you why I was only offering so much for the watch because it didn't work, whereas the rug was of good quality and in fine condition.'

'What if a stranger brings in a necklace, or medals from the Boer War?' she fretted. 'If there is anything you really don't know about ask them to come back another day.

'I am confident you will have come across most items and you can always compare it with other things in the shop.'

'I will try,' Ester agreed. 'I've always wondered what it would be like to be the other side of the counter!' She laughed.

'Don't be giving away all my money!' he joked.

Ester glanced at her blackened copper kettle and wished she had some refreshment to offer him.

'Come in early on Wednesday so I can get a carriage in good time,' Adam said.

He reached in his pocket and produced

a small book which instantly caught the interest of both Polly and Ester.

'Look at this. It's 'The Tale Of Peter Rabbit'. A lady called Beatrix Potter has written the story and drawn the pictures.

'I already have a buyer for it but I wanted to show it to you both first.'

Adam read the story and showed Polly the pictures as reverently as though they were stories from the Bible.

'More!' Polly kept saying. Even Bertie the bunny had been abandoned momentarily.

'I am told there are five more books but I have not seen them myself. I rarely get to see such beautiful things.

'If I were rich I would collect books, not just picture books but those with maps. I'd like to read adventure stories and to learn all about Greek gods and times gone by.'

'Oh, Adam, this is the most beautiful treasure I have ever seen! Thank you for sharing it with us.'

'It is one of the perks of the trade.' He smiled. 'Now and again I am offered something really interesting.

'My cousin and I usually share these rare finds. Robert has a buyer for this one.'

'You'd have loved my father's study, Adam. It was full of medical books. I was fascinated even as a child.'

Ester looked down at her hands.

'They were all sold with the house to pay off the debts.'

'Not sad face, Mummy!' Polly entreated and instantly Ester's face brightened up.

'Shall we look at Peter Rabbit once more?' Adam suggested. 'Do you think he looks a bit like Bertie?'

On Wednesday Ester arrived at the Emporium bearing Polly and her sewing.

Adam showed her where a few things were and had even bought them bread and jam to eat.

'I'll be back as soon as I can,' he promised. 'But it's a long journey, even if my meeting is brief. I also plan to visit my dear aunt, Maud. She lives nearby but I don't see her as often as I'd like.'

'Don't worry, I'll look after things as best I can,' Ester reassured him.

Having looked around his shop more closely she was now feeling more confident.

A Welcome Sight

The morning was quiet. One customer came in to buy a hat and Ester not only sold him the hat but a pair of gloves as well.

The afternoon was a different story. The bell on the entrance door tinkled frequently as customers used their afternoon off to pawn small items or to redeem those they'd pawned the previous week.

Ester wished Adam had been present because she had to keep an eye on the customers in the shop as well as serve the person in front of her.

It was time to close up. Adam had not returned but Ester decided to wait for him. It was warm in the shop and she was keen to see him and to hear about his day.

He'd not gone into any details about his errand but he would probably tell her about his journey and what he'd seen.

The bell tinkled and Ester sighed.

She'd been keen to lock up so she could relax.

It had been such a responsibility to look after the business for Adam. Most of the customers had been polite, especially when she treated them with the respect Adam would have given.

One or two of the men had insisted they'd only deal with Adam and would come back when he was in. It was to be expected and she took no offence.

'Can I help?' Ester asked a woman who was hovering near the door.

After a few moments she left the counter and went to see if she needed assistance.

'Ann!' She gasped as the woman straightened up.

Her friend's face was bruised but she wore a big smile.

'Don't hug me too tightly,' she warned. Her chest rattled as she breathed. 'I've been in the wars meself, but I'm back now.

'I was told I'd find you in here.'

'Come in. Adam's not home,' Ester

said. 'Let me lock up and I'll make you some tea and supper.'

'Adam, is it, now?' Ann mocked. 'Since when has Mr Boniface been Adam?'

'Never mind that,' Ester scolded her. 'You disappeared without trace and all we found was your coat!'

'You found my coat?'

Ann looked surprised, then frowned.

'Where is everyone? I went home and there's another family living in my house now!'

Attacked!

'My, she's grown,' Ann said as she looked at Polly playing in a corner.

'Tell me what happened,' Ester begged. 'Then I'll fill you in on our news.'

Ann explained how she'd left the Manor House with a full stomach, a basket of food and her wages hidden in her boots. It made walking difficult but was safer that way.

'I'd not gone far when I had a feeling I was being followed.'

She glanced over in Polly's direction and continued with her story in a hushed voice.

'Someone attacked me from behind! I think I fought back because I had a handful of yellow hair in my fist when I was found.'

'Found?' Ester asked.

'The knock on the head made me confused and I must have wandered around all night.

'I remember feeling cold, as I had no

78

coat, so I curled up in a barn. The farmer and his wife found me in the morning and looked after me.

'The head injury made me drift in and out of consciousness.'

'You've been missing for ages!'

'The farmer's wife nursed me till I was physically well but I couldn't remember who I was or where I'd come from.

'They called me Rosemary because they'd had a daughter by that name who'd died. I worked with them on the farm and, slowly, I started remembering things.'

'What sort of things?' Ester asked.

'Well, I kept asking for people called Bobby and Mary although I didn't know who they were.

'Then, one day, the farmer's wife mentioned a lady called Ann and I knew that was my name.'

Ann finished her cup of tea.

'Where are the children?'

'I did my best, honest I did, Ann,' Ester said with tears in her eyes. 'But we were running out of food and I had no money left.

'Then your husband returned and . . .'

'He's back?' Ann gasped. 'No-one said.'

'He thanked me for looking after them and gave me a locket he said he'd brought back for you.

'I needed money for rent so I pawned it but Constable Harris saw it and said it was stolen. I refused to say where I'd got it so I was put in prison!'

'No!'

'It was horrid, I can tell you. I missed Polly so much. I never felt I'd ever actually be charged because I knew I was innocent.

'Perhaps that was naïve of me, but it gave me hope.'

'And had he stolen it?'

Ann's voice was flat as though she expected she knew the answer. Ester wondered if Leonard had stolen things before.

'I don't know how he came to have it, but eventually he did admit to giving it to me.

'It was after he had had a few pints and lots of people heard him, including Constable Harris. I was released and he was arrested.'

'And the children?' Ann asked again urgently.

'Adam told me he found Mary in the workhouse. She was being fed and had a roof over her head.'

'What about Bobby?' Ann's voice had a wobble in it.

'Bobby has had a real growth spurt!' Ester replied, smiling. 'He looks older than his years and he has been working in the woods, chopping up logs and selling them.

'There was a group of men who have a camp in the forest. I think he's still there with them.

'They get paid on a Friday and most of them come into town for a drink at the King's Head. Adam always buys Bobby a pie and checks he's all right.'

Ann nodded.

'As soon as I've got work I'll go and fetch Mary back. Can I stay with you until I get myself sorted?' she asked.

Ester smiled.

'You know what the landlord says — no subletting. But you can stay with me tonight so long as you're gone by morning and no-one sees you go.'

'Thanks, Ester, you're a good friend.'

A short while later Adam returned home. Ann made her excuses and under cover of darkness went off to sleep in Ester's small room.

'I'll just catch up here and then I'll come and join you,' Ester told her.

'Shall I take Polly back and put her to bed?' Ann asked.

'No, that's fine,' Ester said quickly.

She knew Ann wasn't strong enough yet to carry Polly to the door of the shop, let alone all the way home.

'You go and make yourself comfy and I'll be home soon.'

A Reward

Once Ann had gone Ester filled Adam in on the transactions she'd made on his behalf during the day.

She was thrilled to tell him about the man who came in for a hat and went away with hat and gloves.

'Did you have any time to sew?'

'I made good progress this morning and everything is hanging on the rail for you to check. I hoped to clear some space in the window to display them, but as you said, it was very busy this afternoon.'

'I'll take a proper look at things tomorrow when the light's better,' Adam told her.

'Now, let me tell you about my day. Constable Harris charged me with the job of returning the locket to Lady Greenway.

'She lives some distance away but I had business in that direction and had a profitable day.'

'Go on,' Ester urged.

'Lady Greenway was delighted to see her locket again. It had belonged to her mother, who had died in childbirth, and so was very precious.

'The locket meant a great deal — so much so she insisted on giving me a reward!'

'A reward?'

Ester was happy for him.

'I told her how I came to have it in my possession and she was very sympathetic towards you.

'She has given me two purses. One for me, because I took the trouble to return her locket, and one for you for the trouble it caused you. She was adamant about this.'

Adam reached into his coat and pulled out a small purse which he handed over to Ester.

'I owe you for your time here today and for your work on these garments. Perhaps you'll call by tomorrow and we can sort out what I need to pay you.'

'But . . .'

'It's what we agreed,' Adam said firmly. 'You just need to think about whether you want me to speak to my cousin Robert about the Singer sewing-machine he has acquired, or whether you use this money to begin your medical training.'

Ester's jaw dropped. Not only had Adam taken her seriously about her ambitions but he was also offering her the chance to make her dreams come true!

She could have kissed him! But, of course, that would not be seemly.

Instead she gathered up Polly and headed home, promising to call in again in the morning when they would discuss the matter further.

'Could you keep my money safe?' she begged. 'I dare not take it back with me.

'I trust Ann but what if her husband turned up or I was attacked on my way home?'

'I will keep it secure for you,' Adam assured her. 'I shall also escort you home, as any gentleman should do. Do you think Polly will let me carry her?'

That night, as Ester cradled her daughter in her arms, she tried to sleep.

Ann's chest rattled as she slept. They had no mattress and the stone floor was cold and hard. Noises could be heard above them and from outside.

Ester closed her eyes. All she could think of was Adam Boniface, standing tall and handsome in front of her.

The image of his open and honest face kept coming back to her.

It was so clear she could almost reach out and stroke his cheek, caress his lips and feel his strong arms around her, holding her close and loving her.

Foolish Jealousy

Ester was up early the following day having slept surprising well. This was partly due to the warmth of Ann's body nearby but more because of her good fortune.

She decided not to say anything to anyone. Folk could be funny about others coming into reward money. Sometimes it was best to keep good news to yourself.

On her way to the Emporium she called in on Mrs Brown who ran two clothing establishments almost single-handedly.

'I've done your mending.' Ester handed over the garments she'd worked on.

Mrs Brown picked them up and inspected them carefully.

'Your stitches are so tiny I can hardly see them! You did well. I'll use you again.'

'I've been doing alterations on some dresses. Would you be interested in having a look?' Ester asked. 'I could bring them over this afternoon.'

'I'll be interested in seeing them but I'm not making any promises.'

Ester hurried off to meet Adam, clutching the coins Mrs Brown had given her. Were things beginning to look up for her at last?

At the shop Adam had already worked out what he owed her for her time and had given each garment a new price.

'I think Mrs Brown may be interested in one of the dresses,' she told him. 'I said I'd take them over this afternoon.

'I didn't tell her where I'd got them from. Perhaps it's best that way.'

'As you say.' Adam nodded. 'Have you had a chance to consider your options?'

'I've hardly thought of anything else,' Ester confessed, although she had also thought a great deal about Adam Boniface himself and his kindness.

'I am not in a position to begin any medical training,' she added. 'Can you tell me more about this sewing-machine?'

'I thought you would make that decision so I took the liberty of sending a note to my cousin. He'll deliver it tomorrow morning when he's in this area.' Adam smiled.

'I'm not familiar with one. What if I don't get on with it?' Ester asked in sudden panic. 'Maybe I should save my money.'

'There is no obligation on you to buy. You can have a look at it and try it. Robert is asking five pounds, four shillings for cash. It's a three-quarter-sized machine which makes it quite portable.

'But you ought to see it for yourself.'

Excited at the thought of seeing the sewing-machine the following day, Ester collected up the garments to take to Mrs Brown and thanked Adam again.

Mrs Brown was busy with her sister when Ester arrived with the dresses. She asked her to leave them and to call back later.

Ester hesitated but decided to do as they asked.

As she shopped for food in the market she kept an eye open for Ann but didn't catch sight of her.

She wished her friend well and hoped she was successful in finding work.

A little later she returned to Mrs Brown's and was delighted to learn that two of the five dresses had already been sold.

She took the money back to Adam in the hope he'd remember they had agreed to make a 50-50 split.

On entering the shop she was surprised to find Adam behind his counter deep in conversation with an elegant woman.

He didn't even turn when the door-bell chimed, which was unusual.

Ester was disappointed. She always looked forward to seeing Adam's face light up with a smile at the sight of her.

At least, that was what she'd thought.

Now she watched as the elegant lady he was listening to touched his arm gently and together they laughed at some little joke.

How foolish she felt, to think that the likes of Adam Boniface could ever be interested in a simple girl like her!

He was of a certain standing in the

community and he mixed with far more important people than the likes of Ester Sharp. Only recently he'd been in the company of Lady Greenway!

She bit back tears, filled with anger at making a fool of herself and, she had to admit, with an overwhelming feeling of jealousy.

Now she accepted that Adam Boniface was a lovely man who was always courteous and respectful to all and sundry.

He was kindness itself, and never a day went by without him having done a good deed for someone.

She was lucky to work alongside him and had been foolish to think he treated her any differently from all his other customers.

He was just a kind man and she had been lucky to benefit from his charity.

Adam and the lady were still deep in conversation. Neither of them even noticed she was there.

Ester hated this feeling of being invisible, especially when only yesterday she had felt so important and even special in his eyes.

Especially in his eyes.

She gave a little cough to draw attention to herself. It worked — the two of them looked over in her direction.

'Ah, here is Mrs Sharp, the lady I was telling you about,' Adam said.

He spoke with this other woman in a friendly and familiar tone, just like the way he spoke with Ester. It was as though she were a friend.

However, he'd not introduced Ester as his business partner and that, she felt, didn't bode well.

'Ester, will you show Miss Clara the garments you've been working on?'

'I've sold two of them already,' Ester told him quietly.

She had been so pleased with herself but now, for some stupid reason, she felt embarrassed by the whole situation.

Little Polly pulled at her skirt and kept pointing up at Bertie who was sitting high up on a shelf, out of reach.

Usually Adam reached for the toy as

soon as Polly entered the shop but today his head seemed to have been turned by the lovely Miss Clara.

Ester was about to hand over the money with the dresses but hesitated. She didn't want to conduct their private business in front of this strange woman.

Instead, she held out one of the dresses and while Miss Clara was examining it, just as Mrs Brown had done, Ester asked if Polly could play with Bertie.

'Of course.' Adam said instantly and reached up to lift him down. 'Here you are.'

Polly gave him a big smile just as she always did. Usually their interaction warmed Ester's heart but today it made her feel sad.

'May I borrow Mrs Sharp for a moment?' Miss Clara asked Adam.

Ester looked from one to the other. She wanted to object and point out that she was neither his property nor a member of his staff but his equal, his business partner.

'Did you wish to show me something?'

Ester asked the lady, trying to keep her voice even.

Miss Clara led her to a dark corner of the shop. Ester had never had a chance to browse here because she always had Polly to keep an eye on.

As they walked away from the counter Ester wondered if perhaps Miss Clara was not intending to show her anything, but wished instead to warn her to keep her hands off the eligible and handsome Mr Boniface!

A Special Dress

'Have you seen this?' Miss Clara asked as they reached a clothes rail. She pulled out a bundle of muslin and lace. 'Let's get it into the light and see what condition it's in.'

Ester gasped. The dress was a beautiful wedding dress. It reminded her of the one she herself had worn when her father had walked her down the aisle.

'It's lovely,' she replied, trying to keep her voice calm.

'Yes, and it's in better condition that I thought it would be. It used to be hanging up and it caught my attention some years ago, when I first came in here with my brother.

'I suppose it must have fallen down behind the rail. Is it repairable, do you think?'

It was Ester's turn to examine the dress. To her it seemed to be in very good condition.

She began to wonder if this was some

sort of test, to see if she would pretend it needed alterations when none were necessary.

'Other than needing a good airing it appears in good condition,' Ester declared, feeling it was better to stick with the truth.

'But isn't it rather dated?' Miss Clara suggested. 'It's been hanging up for at least the last five years!'

'A well-made, classic wedding gown, such as this, is timeless. I don't think it would need any alterations unless the customer wanted to add a personal touch.'

'Such as?'

'Well, if a bride wanted to add a pale blue ribbon, for example, I could weave one along here and on the sleeves.'

'Like the poem? Something old, something new, something borrowed . . .' Miss Clara quoted.

'Something blue and a silver sixpence in my shoe.' Ester finished the rhyme. 'I could even create a spider's web design to hold a sixpence on the top of each shoe.'

'You could do that?' Miss Clara looked amazed. 'That's a wonderful idea! Where did you see that?'

'I haven't. I just thought about it. The shoes would have to be right, of course, and I'd need to find the perfect matching silk thread.'

'Interesting,' Miss Clara said thoughtfully. 'Are there any shoes in here?'

Ester wasn't sure why they were having this conversation.

'The locals usually just trade in old boots.' She gave a little laugh.

Miss Clara seemed quite serious, however.

'Actually, I have seen a pair,' Ester mused. 'They're pale green, the wrong colour for this gown, but the style is perfect. Perhaps they could be bleached.'

She hurried to the counter where Polly was sitting quietly with Bertie the rabbit. She was rocking him in her arms and singing him to sleep.

'Here!' Ester picked up and dusted off a small pair of lady's silk shoes. 'Supposing these were the right colour we could stitch a silver sixpence right there in the centre. If that was what the bride wanted.'

Just then the door to the shop burst open, letting in a cloud of smoke and the strong smell of burning.

'The King's Head's on fire!' a man shouted from the doorway. 'Have you got anything that carries water?'

Adam snapped into action and in no time at all found coal scuttles, buckets and a tin bath.

He removed his jacket, rolled up his sleeves and went outside to help put out the fire.

Ester prayed no-one would be hurt, least of all Adam.

A Blackened Shell

The smell of smoke still hung in the air the following morning when Ester went to see if Mr Boniface's cousin had delivered the sewing-machine.

'I thought you'd be in bright and early,' Adam said with a cheery welcome. 'Have you seen the King's Head? It's just a shell now. Still, no-one was hurt.'

'It'll be missed. All sorts of people did their business there. I don't know where they'll go now.'

Ester wanted to suggest that the men could stay at home, as their wives did. But she had no wish to pick an argument with the one person who took her seriously.

The Singer sewing-machine sat on a little table. Her first impression was that it was in good condition. It had a wooden cover with a key and a handle and, in theory, she could carry it from place to place.

'I have it on good authority that these

are sturdy and reliable machines. I'll fetch you a chair and some scraps of material if you wish to try it out.'

'You realise I've never used one of these before?' Ester reminded Adam.

'I thought your mother was a seam-stress?' he asked.

'She was but she did everything by hand. I am sure she would dearly have loved to own a sewing-machine.'

Two gentlemen came in to speak with Adam which left Ester to have a closer look at the sewing-machine and to figure out how it worked.

She turned the handle slowly, noting it made the needle go up and down.

Adam had left her some material and his mother's workbasket which con-tained thread.

Her first few attempts were not good. The first was far too loose and the stitches soon unravelled.

Her second attempt was the opposite — far too tight, which caused the mate-rial to curl up. Everything became tangled.

She removed this second try and found another small piece of material.

'How is it going?' Adam asked as the two gentlemen he'd been talking to left.

'I'm beginning to get the hang of it. I don't think I would use it for everything but I can see some situations where it would be much quicker if I used the machine.'

'Well, then, am I to put a label on it marked 'sold'?'

He smiled, his old, kindly self again instead of the aloof man he'd been yesterday.

'I have to give it a bit more thought,' Ester told him as she tried to weigh up the advantages and disadvantages.

If she invested in this machine it could earn her more money which would, in turn, help her make something of herself and provide better for Polly.

At that moment she heard Polly cough. She had been doing this a lot since the fire.

The strong smell of smoke irritated the eyes and tickled the throat. It made your clothes and your hair smell of burned wood.

'Good day to you, Adam,' Ester called as she scooped up Polly.

'Off so soon?'

'This air is making her cough. I want to see how far we need to go before we can't smell it any more.'

Holding Polly's hand she walked and walked until eventually the air seemed less heavy with smoke and Polly stopped rubbing her eyes.

They explored the area for a while until it began to rain. On their way back they went through an unfamiliar market place.

There were several shops all around the square. They all looked inviting and Ester realised the little money she had was burning a hole in her pocket. The sooner she spent it on something useful and worthwhile, the better.

The rain was becoming heavier which helped to clear the air but made them cold. They took cover in doorways and gradually made their way back to their part of town.

The building that had once been the King's Head, and which was the liveliest place on a Friday evening when the men had been paid, was now a blackened shell.

A few charred beams remained in place but the roof had caved in. It was all barricaded off as it was no longer safe.

Ester returned to the Emporium to find Miss Clara visiting again. She was looking at the sewing-machine.

'I've decided I will buy it,' Ester told Adam. 'May I collect it tomorrow?'

'I can deliver it, if you like.'

Ester felt there was no sense prolonging her heartbreak. It was clear he was destined to be with Miss Clara.

'That's kind but there is no need,' she told him in what she hoped was a businesslike voice. 'Perhaps you'll have some time tomorrow to go through a few more garments with me?'

'Certainly,' he said as he opened the door to let them off the premises and back out into the pouring rain.

Community Spirit

The publican of the King's Head rented a couple of rooms so he could carry on his business.

He and his partner had managed to save the barrels of beer and had made numerous journeys to and fro to see what else they could salvage.

Word soon spread around the area that a make-shift inn was about to open.

The beer was ready, the room had been swept but somehow it was not the same.

'There's no atmosphere,' one of the men mourned to Adam Boniface the following day. 'We need tables and chairs, horse-brasses for the wall, benches to sit on and a bell to call last orders.'

'I can't help you with furniture,' Adam told him, 'but my cousin Robert has a barn full of stuff that he'd be pleased to get rid of. I'll send word to him.'

He wandered around the Emporium.

'I'm sure I've got a bell here somewhere.'

At last he found a ship's bell.

'Will that do?'

There was a hive of activity over the next few days. A wagon was borrowed from Whitecross Farm to collect several items of furniture to refurbish the temporary inn.

There was a commotion going on inside the pawnbroker's shop when Ester arrived to collect her sewing-machine and to discuss some extra work with Adam.

Mrs Brown was at the counter, banging her fist on it to show her disapproval on some matter.

Ester immediately thought of the dresses she'd altered. She wondered if she should have said they'd been pawned previously.

'Ah, Mrs Sharp, you've come for your sewing-machine,' Adam said by way of greeting. 'Allow me to carry it for you.'

Mrs Brown stormed out and Adam heaved a sigh of relief. He closed the shop and followed Ester as she went to her home.

'What did Mrs Brown want?' she asked.

'I thought I was doing the right thing by donating some furniture to help the landlord get back on his feet.'

'That was very good of you.'

It went to confirm what she already knew; Adam Boniface had a heart of gold and was good to everyone.

'The trouble is, Mrs Brown thinks I am showing favouritism and she doesn't think that's fair.'

'Her inn wasn't burned down!'

'I know, but apparently she's hired a room next to the new inn. It's called the Temperance Room and she's allowing in women.'

'Good for her!'

Although she'd never had any wish to enter the man's world of a public house Ester didn't like the idea that she wouldn't be welcome just because she was a woman.

'You think it a good idea?' Adam was surprised.

'A Temperance Room won't serve

alcohol,' Ester explained. 'I am sure it would be a more sensible and genteel place to visit rather than a public house.'

'Do you think I ought to donate some furniture to her?'

'If you do you'd better make it clear that you have a business to run and you can't keep giving things away! People will always try to get something for nothing.'

Adam considered.

'As it happens, Robert is very keen to get rid of furniture that's been in storage. I do remember padded chairs that would look more in place in a parlour for the ladies.'

'You know Mrs Brown will be very grateful and will send business your way.'

'Mrs Sharp, I do believe you're right!'

Ester looked up at him. Had she dreamed they had once been on first-name terms?

A Neighbour's Misfortune

Ester had a neighbour, Edie, who had three small children. Her husband had volunteered to go and fight for his country in the Great War. There had been a little income when he first signed up but that had now fizzled out.

The weather had been mild for the time of year and Ester had managed to collect some wild herbs which she used to flavour a thin broth to which she added what vegetables she had.

She shared what little she had with Edie and her family.

'I've nothing left to pawn,' the woman told her as she twisted her wedding ring.

'I thought you'd found some work?' Ester asked.

'I have been working but he can't pay me until the goods are sold. It could be next week before I get anything.

'I told him I've got kids to feed but what does he care?'

Ester looked at Edie's bare feet. She'd

already pawned her boots.

'Will yer take my ring and see what you can get for it? Make sure you tell him I'll be in to get it back as soon as I gets paid. Make sure you tell him that.'

'Don't worry, Edie, Mr Boniface will understand.'

Early the next morning Ester took Edie's wedding ring and pawned it on her behalf, explaining that it would be redeemed as soon as her employer paid her.

'I can put it aside for an extra week,' Adam said. 'Would that give her enough leeway?'

'It should do. Thank you for understanding. It's not easy for her, trying to manage on her own with three little ones to feed and clothe.'

★ ★ ★

The plan should have worked well except Edie's husband had been shot in the foot and was sent home until it healed.

Pain was making him bad-tempered.

'He'll kill me if he finds out what I've done!' Edie fretted. 'So far I've managed to hide it from him.'

'You haven't done anything wrong,'

But Ester knew Edie's husband would not see things that way.

'Take mine. He'll not know the difference.'

Ester slipped the ring from her own finger and gave it to her neighbour. It slid easily on Edie's finger and the relief showed instantly in her face.

'Thank you so much!' she said. 'As soon as I get paid I'll get my ring back and return yours. I owe you, Ester, I really do.'

Ester spent the day altering worn old garments and converting them into new, more pleasing outfits better suited for today's times.

It was satisfying work and by the afternoon she felt she'd mastered her new machine. She had made the right decision in purchasing it.

Using it was certainly quicker than sewing by hand. It was also easier on her fingers.

Having been cooped up all day sewing, with only two-year-old Polly to talk to, she decided she would run round to the pawnshop and return the garments to Adam Boniface before he shut.

Once again it had been raining for most of the day but, now that it had stopped, it had cleared away the smoke from the fire. Now there only the familiar smell of logs burning in hearths, which Ester hardly noticed.

Polly was pleased to walk out with her mother and was trying to skip as Mary had been teaching her. She hadn't quite mastered it but she was in a happy mood.

Ester, too, felt like skipping. She'd spent a productive day and had something to show for it.

Hopefully Adam would be pleased with her work and pay her for her time. He may even have sold an item of clothing that would earn her 50% of the profit.

Many people avoided the Emporium. Ester wondered if the sadness associated with having to trade useful possessions, simply to have money for basic food,

111

tarnished the thrill of visiting his store.

It always took her a few moments to become accustomed to the dimness of the inside of the pawnshop. It was stacked high with other people's belongings, many of which had been there for decades.

As far as she was aware the interior was never dusted and it was not possible to get near enough to the windows to give them a clean.

In fairness, she had no other pawnshop to compare it with, although she had briefly caught a glimpse of Cousin Robert's shop when she had collected Polly.

Robert's shop looked almost identical. If anything, Adam did at least try to group similar items together to make it easier to find things.

Adam was not standing behind the counter as usual but Ester could hear his voice. He and a customer were discussing the qualities of a painting on the other side of the shop.

She hoped he'd make a sale.

Ester realised she had been holding her breath, wondering if she'd find Miss Clara in situ.

'Only me!' she called out.

Polly had already rushed over to the counter and was looking around to find Bertie.

'Don't worry, Polly, I'll get him.'

While the child was playing with Bertie, showing him all the things at her eye level in the shop, Ester arranged her garments on a rail near the counter where they could be noticed easily.

She sighed when she finished because she realised that most of the women who entered the shop were there out of desperation.

Their only concern was to feed and clothe their children. They had no use for lace-collared dresses.

Occasionally a gentleman would come in to buy a trinket for a lady friend.

Only husbands bought their wives items of clothing, and then it was on impulse and usually as an apology.

More Misfortune

Adam was in a good mood, having sold two paintings and a piano.

'I didn't know you had a piano!' Ester said in surprise. 'Where was that hidden away?'

He gestured to an area near the exit. Ester couldn't help but smile. She had used that door many times — how could she possibly not have noticed a piano?

He was just about to examine her latest creations when they heard the doorbell chime and looked up.

No-one entered but it was clear some-one was still outside.

'I'll go,' Ester told him and headed for the door.

Edie was outside, looking furtive.

'What's wrong?'

'I've lost it!' her neighbour cried and waved her ringless hand. 'One minute it was there; the next, gone! I've searched and searched.'

'Where were you?'

'I don't know exactly where I lost it,' Edie managed to say between sobs. 'I've looked everywhere at home but it could have been in the town when I queued for bread.'

Ester managed to draw the woman into the shop and settle her down on a chair. Quickly she explained the situation to Adam Boniface.

'I had noticed you weren't wearing your ring,' he said to Ester's surprise.

'May I make Edie a hot, sweet tea to calm her down?' she begged.

'Shouldn't she be looking for your ring?' he asked instead as he glanced over at Edie who had stopped crying. 'And where are her children?'

'They're out hunting for the ring,' Edie supplied. 'Everyone is! Not a word to my husband, mind. There will be hell to pay if he ever finds out.'

She stood, shook herself down and headed for the door.

'I'm so sorry, Ester. I don't know when I can pay you back but I will, somehow.'

Ester watched her go. The poor woman

was in a worse state than before. She had only pawned her original ring to tide her over until her employer had paid her.

Now, when she got paid and she could retrieve her own wedding ring, she would have to give Ester something for the loss of the loaned ring.

But Edie wasn't in a position to do that at the moment, Ester was certain. There had been times when she herself had considered pawning her wedding ring but for her it had not yet come to that.

She knew she was lucky because she'd been able to be more resourceful than many of her neighbours.

Having had an education had helped her even if it had alienated her at times, too.

She just didn't belong anywhere.

'Have you a moment to look at my work?' Ester asked Adam, trying to be as businesslike as possible. 'If it's not con-venient now I can come back later.'

'I'm sure your work is fine,' he said. 'How many hours do I owe you?'

'Three.'

'Are you sure?' He looked up from the ledger on his desk.

'Yes. Using the sewing-machine has speeded things up so much. I don't use it for everything but it makes a very good hem in half the time.'

'Well, if you're sure.' He made a note before reaching into his cashbox for a few coins.

'Thank you,' she said, accepting the money. 'I'll just find a few more garments and then Polly and I ought to go and help to look for my ring.'

'There is no need to take anything else at the moment,' Adam told her.

This made her stop suddenly and look back at him.

'The agreement was, if I am not mistaken, that you were to work on five original garments and we would assess things once they had sold.'

Ester gulped, realising her enthusiasm had swept her along.

Having sold two dresses to Mrs Brown and receiving compliments on her work from Miss Clara she had become carried away.

'You are correct, of course,' she managed to say. 'Forgive me if I have overstepped the mark.'

'I understand that you are keen and that is a good thing, but in business we have to be cautious,' he replied. 'There is no point spending money on items that will not prove worthy.'

'I know what you mean.' She hesitated for a moment. 'I am sure I can improve the quality of some of the outfits you have, however. That, for example.'

Ester pointed at a pale green evening dress. From the style it had been made some time ago and, no doubt, had been handed down more than once.

'I'm not disagreeing with you, Mrs Sharp,' Adam said, 'but at the moment I cannot justify the speculation.'

Ester picked up her shopping basket without another word, reached for Polly's hand and left the Emporium.

She had enough money in her purse to pay the rent and buy food for them both. What more could she want?

Polly was quiet as they walked to the town to buy victuals. Ester looked at her daughter.

Neither she nor Adam Boniface had raised their voices but perhaps Polly had picked up on their disagreement. Could a child so young do that?

It had not been lost on Ester that they had slipped back into their formal ways. He had referred to her as Mrs Sharp.

The more she thought back over their conversation the more cross it made her.

Perhaps she had gone too far to expect to be allowed to make Edie a cup of hot, sweet tea to calm her.

But the Adam Boniface she thought she knew was a kind and generous man. In fact, he seemed to go to extraordinary lengths at times to help people in distress.

For no reason other than her own jealousy she blamed Miss Clara for his change of heart.

Ever since that woman had arrived he had changed, and not for the better!

Running Away

'Ann, is that you?'

Ester had recognised the back of a tall, thin woman who was peering into a shop window.

Ann Granger turned and smiled.

'Ester!'

'I've been looking out for you every day,' Ester told her friend. 'You seemed to have disappeared! Have you been reunited with your Bobby?'

'I've seen him. He's been earning good money chopping wood so, for the moment, I've let him be.'

'What about yourself? Have you found work?'

'There's nothing at the factory. I did go to see Mrs Walcot at the Manor House but everything is quiet there as the entire family has gone to London.

'They might not even come back for Christmas so I'm not needed at the moment.'

'Oh, dear.'

Ester wanted to ask about young Mary. Did Ann's daughter remain in the workhouse?

'I did go to visit the farmer and his wife,' Ann went on. 'Those who found me when I had been attacked.

'I know I wasn't with them very long but they felt like family to me. Would you believe it? They have said I can have a home with them!'

'On the farm?'

Ester was surprised her town-reared friend was even considering this option.

'Yes. They're not as strong as they used to be and they have said they could find work for Bobby as he's young and good with his hands.

'They also said they would give me and Mary a home, too, as long as we pulled our weight. We can all sleep in the loft over the barn.'

'Is that what you're going to do?'

Ester would be sorry to see her friend leave after having lost her for so long, but would understand her decision.

She would do the same if it meant

keeping her family together.

Ann nodded, smiling.

'I'm just off to fetch Mary from the workhouse. Bobby will join us on Friday after he's been paid.

'I know I'm running away but I think it's for the best. Don't tell anyone where I've gone, will you?'

'I shan't say a word.'

Ester squeezed her friend's arm.

'I suppose I'll have to call you Rosemary from now on!' she whispered which made Ann smile.

'That you will. I'm sad to go but it's for the best.'

'God bless you.' Ester gave her a hug. 'For what it's worth I think you've made the right decision, but I shall miss you.'

'You've got Adam now.'

'Mr Boniface has a new friend. She's called Miss Clara and I'm back to being plain old Mrs Sharp.'

'Oh, no! What happened?' Ann shook her head in dismay.

'Nothing except that Miss Clara is beautiful and elegant and probably doesn't live in a shared tenant building with a small child!'

'Don't be too hard on yourself,' Ann advised. 'Take care.'

The two friends went their separate ways. Ester was happy for Ann and it gave her renewed hope that good things could and did happen for good people.

An Invitation

Two weeks passed before Ester had cause to revisit Adam Boniface in his shop.

There had been no sign of her lost wedding ring. It was generally thought to have slipped through the floorboards or have been found in a gutter by someone else.

Edie was avoiding Ester, no doubt because she still felt guilty and knew she was in her debt.

'Mrs Sharp!' Adam said as soon as Ester stepped foot in the pawnshop. 'I wondered if you were still angry with me.'

'I was angry with myself,' Ester confessed. 'You were correct. Our original agreement had been to sell all five garments.

'I was enjoying the sewing so much, I believe, that enthusiasm got the better of me.'

'I have good news for you, as it happens.'

He reached into his desk and pulled out an envelope which had her name on it.

'Two more garments have sold!'

'Really?'

Ester was surprised. They had been on a rack near the counter and she had doubted that the right customers would ever see them.

'I'm delighted!'

She looked around for the rail but couldn't see it anywhere.

'I'm glad you've come in,' Adam was saying. 'There is something I've been wanting to ask you.'

Ester was only half listening as she searched around for the last outfit.

She wanted to bring it to the forefront of the shop so it had the best chance of being seen and thus sold.

'Are you listening to me?'

'Sorry.' She stopped and looked directly at him. 'What were you saying?'

'I've been given tickets for a motion picture being shown at the Picture Palace. I was wondering if you'd like to accompany me.'

'Me?' This was probably the last thing she had expected.

'Me?' Polly's voice echoed in the background.

Ester chuckled at her daughter but it reminded her there was no way she could accept his invitation.

She was after all, a woman with responsibilities.

'That's very kind of you, but I can't accept,' she told him.

Mr Boniface looked thoughtful as he rearranged the watches on display.

'Do you dislike the picture palaces?' he asked.

'I have never been. I did love going to the music halls with my father.'

'Is it me you dislike, then?'

She looked up and he softened his tone.

'I would like you to come. In fact, I was so sure you would enjoy it I approached my favourite aunt, Maud, and asked if she would look after Polly.'

Ester was dumbfounded. This invitation had caught her unawares. It surprised her that he had considered Polly but why hadn't he asked Miss Clara to go with him?

'Isn't there someone else you would rather take?'

'No,' he replied. 'I am disappointed. I thought you would be pleased and I looked forward to sharing my good fortune. Perhaps I shall offer to take Aunt Maud.'

She could hear the hurt in his voice.

'That sounds like a good idea.' Ester said quietly. 'I've been asked to pawn these. My friend hopes to redeem them by the end of the week when her husband is paid.'

She produced a pair of pillowcases.

Adam wrote out the details then handed over a few coppers and the slip of paper.

'Polly,' Ester called. 'Time to go.'

'Why, Mummy?' Polly was beginning to question more and more.

'Perhaps we could start again,' Adam said. 'May I explain how I come to have these tickets in the first place?'

Polly went back to her building blocks so Ester nodded.

'A short while ago a film-maker came in with a list of props he needed for a motion-picture. Some items were quite unusual but, with the help of my cousin, I managed to find everything on his list.

'He was delighted and paid us well at the time. I thought that was the end of it.'

Adam smiled and he and Ester both looked in Polly's direction but she was engrossed in rearranging the blocks for Bertie the bunny to lie upon.

'Much to my surprise, the film-maker returned with another list of items he is in need of for his next picture.

'He told me how pleased he was with my service on the previous occasion and offered me four tickets — two for myself and two for my cousin.

'They are the best tickets, for a box on our own high up in the gods.'

Ester nodded in understanding and waited for him to continue.

'Is it that you don't think you have

anything to wear?' he asked, suddenly anxious. 'Forgive me, I hadn't even considered that.

'I do know ladies like to dress up when they go out.'

Ester's eyes clouded. It had been many years since she had been out, either for dinner or to the theatre.

She had spent all her time caring for her widowed mother and then, when she had become widowed herself, there had been no money left in the pot.

Adam was searching for something on his desk. He produced a bunch of keys and opened a little safe which was hidden away in the corner, out of sight.

'Please take this. There should be enough for an elegant gown and accessories for the evening.

'You might try Moffat's in Chandlers Lane.'

'Oh, no, I couldn't possibly take that!' Ester replied quickly. 'It wouldn't be right. But I would be more than happy to try on that pale-green gown over there.'

'I agree that would be a good colour

for you,' Adam Boniface responded. 'But first I insist you go to Moffat's.'

Miss Clara

In the end Ester gave in to Adam, especially when he suggested she timed her shopping spree to coincide with his aunt visiting and meeting Polly, just to see how well they got along.

'I really have no choice,' she told herself.

She had no intention, however, of spending Adam's money on an extravagant dress she would wear but once. Especially when there was a perfectly good one she could borrow from the Emporium!

Having said that, she was still looking forward to having an excuse to visit the little boutique in Chandlers Lane.

She had passed it many times and had peered in with Ann. They had laughed together about when they would ever have an opportunity to wear a pretty gown.

All they ever demanded were simple dresses which were practical and modest.

Moffat's was a bow-fronted dress shop for ladies. It sat between a tobacconist and a pharmacy.

When Ester set foot inside the first shock she received was to find Miss Clara serving an elderly customer and her niece.

It was a revelation to discover Miss Clara was, in fact, a working girl.

Ester watched the girl until their eyes met. Miss Clara smiled at her.

'Sorry to keep you, I won't be too long.'

She smiled back, suddenly warming to the girl. No wonder she always looked elegant if she worked in a dress shop!

Ester glanced around the room and took it all in, thinking what she would do if she owned a similar establishment.

For a start, she thought, the room was too dark despite the large bow window at the front.

The walls were dark, too, and the lamp dull in her opinion. Still, Ester was not there to assess the interior of the shop.

She glanced at the rail. A price tag

caught her eye and she gasped.

Although Adam had been more than generous she could not bring herself to spend all that money on a single dress.

Her eye was drawn to another rail tucked away further at the back of the shop. It had a small sign on which was written elegantly in italics, 'Used'.

Ester was drawn to one item in particular because of its familiar fabric.

When she looked closely she knew for sure it was one of the items she had updated for Adam.

Had Miss Clara bought it from him only to display it in her own shop? On further inspection Ester spotted the other garments she'd worked on.

Did that mean Miss Clara had bought them all? If that were the case Adam owed her a percentage.

Also the agreement had been that, if they all sold — which it appeared they had — he would consider commissioning her to work on other garments.

The other customers were leaving and Miss Clara turned her attention to Ester.

Just as they were about to speak Ester read the price attached to one of the old dresses she had updated.

'Is this correct?' Ester asked her in surprise.

'It is,' Miss Clara confirmed. 'If I thought you were really interested in it I would suggest we could agree a price as it has been worn before.'

Ester didn't know what to say. The difference between Adam's price tag and what she saw here was enormous.

Someone was making a lot of money out of her handiwork — and it wasn't her.

'Was there something you were looking for?' Miss Clara asked. 'Or did you just drop by to say hello?'

'I have been invited to the Picture Palace and I fancied a new outfit,' Ester told the girl, slipping into her former persona when she had been respected because her father was a doctor. 'Do you have anything suitable?'

'I would have thought, with your skills, you could design and make something yourself, Mrs Sharp.'

'It is a rather last-minute invitation and I will not have the time,' Ester replied.

She was enjoying the role she was playing. It gave her a pleasant feeling to be back in a world where she was surrounded by beautiful things.

She realised this must have been how her friend, Ann, felt when she'd been in service at the Manor House.

Miss Clara excused herself for a moment and then returned with a silvery gown.

'This is beautiful,' Ester agreed as she felt the softness of the silky fabric.

She held it up against herself in front of the mirror.

'Lovely though the dress is,' she decided, 'it's not for me.'

'A warm gold or a copper is more your colour,' Miss Clara agreed.

Ester was pleased she hadn't been persuaded to buy an unsuitable dress.

Miss Clara offered her a few more to inspect.

'No, the black makes you look too

matronly,' was the verdict. 'And the purple is too heavy. A lilac would work well with your lovely curls but I don't have anything at the moment.'

'I can tell you have a good eye for colour,' Ester told her sincerely.

Indeed, Miss Clara was not only elegant but knew a lot about fashion.

'I think I can confide in you. Did you happen to notice a pale green dress hanging in . . . ?'

'The Emporium?' Miss Clara nodded enthusiastically. 'Now, that definitely is your colour. But I seem to recall it was very long.'

They smiled, both aware that a simple alteration would be easy for Ester to do.

The door chime rang and in walked what looked like a mother and daughter.

Clara and Ester immediately looked at the silver gown that was now draped over the back of a chair.

'Thank you so much for your assistance,' Ester said formally to Clara. 'You have been most helpful and I shall definitely return. Goodbye.'

Dress Fitting

Ester returned promptly to the Emporium. The first thing she heard after the tinkling of the door bell was the sound of Polly's giggles as she sat on Aunt Maud's knee learning a new rhyme.

All well in that department, then.

Adam was showing a gentleman out of the shop. He smiled when he saw her but then frowned to see her empty-handed.

'Didn't you see anything to your fancy?' he asked.

'I saw several interesting garments,' Ester told him, 'but none for me.'

She offered him back the envelope he'd given her.

'There are other boutiques, not just Moffat's, you know.'

'I am aware of that. What I would like to know is how much you would charge me to hire the green dress for one evening, and whether it would be all right if I shortened it?'

'Ester, you know you're very welcome

to take it and to do what you want with it. You don't have to ask!'

'So we are still business partners, is that correct?' she asked, lowering her voice so that Aunt Maud and Polly couldn't hear.

'Yes. Did you think something had changed?'

'I may be wrong,' Ester told him, 'but I believe if we're to be successful business partners then we need to be honest with each other.'

'I couldn't agree more,' Adam told her. 'Shall I reach down this dress for you?'

'Thank you.'

He handed her the pale green dress which, even in the dingy interior of the pawnbroker's, still went well with her coppery curls and pale complexion.

She took the dress and exchanged it for the envelope. Reluctantly Adam took it.

'You do owe me some money, however,' she said quietly. 'I believe the original five garments I amended have all sold.'

'That's what this is all about!' Adam sighed. 'Were they on display at Moffat's?'

'They certainly were and do you have any idea what she was charging for them?'

'The arrangement I have with Miss Clara is that she gets a cut of what she sells on our behalf. You and I split the profit, as we'd agreed.'

'Are you saying she didn't buy them from you?'

He nodded.

'I wish you'd told me about this. She must have seen my shock when I saw them hanging there, not to mention their cost.'

'I'm sorry,' he told her. 'I've never had a business partner before and am used to making my own decisions and acting on them. I didn't think to consult you.

'I thought you'd be pleased. I realise, now, I should have mentioned it.'

Ester felt foolish. She wanted to add she'd also have liked to have been introduced as his business partner to Miss Clara, but now that just sounded petty.

'No harm done,' she said and turned to where Polly was still sitting on Aunt Maud's knee.

She was showing Bertie to the woman.

'Hello,' Aunt Maud greeted her cheerfully. 'I didn't think we were expecting to see you quite so soon. Do show me what you've bought.'

Ester held up the pale green gown for Aunt Maud to inspect.

'What a beautiful colour. It will suit you, I think. Were you fitted?'

'It does need some alteration but I can do that myself.'

'Do you have an assistant to pin it for you?' Aunt Maud probed.

Polly yawned and rubbed her eyes.

'Do you need a little nap, love?'

Polly had made herself a little nest on the floor. Now she curled up on a blanket clutching Bertie.

'If you want to try it on I'll pin it for you, or I could accompany you to your studio.'

It was clear Aunt Maud had no notion of Ester's one-roomed accommodation.

'Actually, that would be very helpful. I would like to see myself in the looking-glass.'

Adam did not have any pins in his shop but he did have wooden pegs which helped Ester determine how much she needed to cut off.

Aunt Maud insisted she changed in his private room while they arranged the looking-glass for when she was ready.

It felt very strange to Ester to be in Adam's personal area and even more odd to be removing her clothes.

However, it was worth it. It was much easier for two people to gauge the correct length of the dress and to decide how best to shorten the sleeves, which were also too long.

After that was sorted Ester was sent home to use her machine before daylight faded. Sewing was never as easy by candlelight.

She altered the hem and sleeves and rushed back to the shop. She knew Polly could become quite irritable when she was hungry.

Fortunately, the child had just woken and they were all keen to see Ester in her new dress.

'Perfect,' Adam said.

Polly clapped her hands.

'Pretty Mummy!' She did a little dance with Bertie.

'Shall I pick you up tomorrow evening?' Adam Boniface asked.

This made Ester panic. She hadn't considered for a moment that Adam's aunt, intended to look after Polly in their miserable little room.

Luckily the older woman came to the rescue.

'Nonsense, you can change at my home, Mrs Sharp. Bring Polly with you and we'll have tea.

'Adam, you can join us, too. We could invite Robert as well and make a little party of it. What do you think?'

Adam told her he thought it was a splendid idea and immediately sent word to his cousin.

At the Picture Palace

Ester ate hardly nothing; she wanted to look her best in her new gown. She stood in front of Aunt Maud's full length looking-glass and studied herself.

There was a tap on the door. Aunt Maud stood in the doorway holding Polly's hand.

'Good, I'm glad I've caught you. I wondered if you wanted to borrow these?'

She handed over a silver trinket box in the shape of a heart.

Ester opened it and gasped. Inside was a dainty necklace with a green stone — an emerald, perhaps — and two matching earrings.

'Try them on,' Aunt Maud urged. 'The minute I saw that dress I knew they'd be just the thing. They've been sitting on my dressing-table since I lost poor George.'

'They could have been made for it,' she said a short while later as they walked down the stairs and into the drawing-room where Adam was waiting with his cousin and wife.

'Thank you so much,' Ester whispered as she gave Aunt Maud a hug. 'I can see why Mr Boniface calls you his favourite aunt! How can I ever repay you?'

Aunt Maud had also unearthed a little fox jacket and dainty slippers ideal for Ester's tiny feet.

'Enjoy your evening!' she called. 'I want to hear all about it in the morning.'

It had been so long since Ester had been dressed up she had to make herself slow down and walk gracefully.

Nowadays she was used to rushing from here to there with her sleeves rolled up and sturdy boots on her feet!

'Relax, Ester,' Adam whispered. 'Polly's in good hands and the evening is young.'

'Are we back to first names again?' she asked, then wished she hadn't. She didn't want anything to spoil the evening.

They were shown to a box with four plush chairs and a small table for their drinks. They were high up to the left of the stage with an excellent view.

Ester glanced down to see the pianist arranging her music and a few other musicians warming up.

A young man was carefully setting out a table of unusual-looking items which would be used to add in the occasional sound effect, such as the sound of a policeman's whistle when he tried to stop a culprit.

Robert's wife, Sophia, was a keen fan of the films. She wanted to know which props had been sourced by the cousins.

'There was a tray, glass decanter and six glasses and also a large water jug,' Adam explained. 'They wanted a hat stand with various large ladies' hats, a gentleman's walking-stick and gloves which had to be white.'

'It's so exciting!' Sophia said as she sipped her Singapore Sling.

'The hardest thing to get hold of was a horn from a Tourer.

'Not the sort of thing that's usually pawned,' he went on. 'I had to go to the car manufacturer in the end.

'Fortunately we'd been allocated a

healthy budget.'

They looked up as the pianist began to play and the lights dimmed.

Ester sat on the edge of her seat, very aware of the warmth from Adam Boniface's body beside her.

He looked dashing in his suit and crisp white shirt. He'd been to the barber's and had polished his shoes.

Ester hoped he wouldn't be a distraction; she had been really looking forward to watching the movie.

Lost and Found

All too soon it was back to reality. Ester hid the green gown in her basket carefully as she returned it to the Emporium. It would not do to reveal such finery to anyone in Tinker's Alley.

She could sense something was amiss as she entered the shop. Adam was pacing up and down, studying something in his hand.

He was so engrossed in what he was doing he wasn't aware of her entering.

'Is something wrong?' she asked as she carefully set Polly down.

He didn't answer her but automatically reached for Bertie and a few other things Polly had taken a shine to recently.

She accepted them happily and only then did he turn to her mother.

He beckoned her to the other side of the long, wooden counter.

'I have a dilemma,' he said and showed her a gold wedding ring in his hand.

'That's mine!' she cried immediately.

'Where did you find it?'

'Are you sure it's yours? To me it looks like any other wedding ring.'

Ester examined it more closely, then slid it on her finger and looked at it once more.

'I am pretty certain it is my ring. It felt right when I put it on and it looks familiar.

'As you say, it is just a gold band. Still, mine had similar dents and scratches, it's the right shape and size and colour and I did lose it recently. Who handed it in?'

'I won't say her name because she may be innocent,' Adam said slowly. 'She had tried, poorly, to disguise herself because I've had trouble with this woman before and have asked her to go elsewhere.'

'That made you suspicious in the first place?'

'It did,' he agreed. 'Added to that, this woman already wore a wedding ring so it wasn't hers.

'I was sure you would recognise it and that it would be a good fit.'

'What are you going to do?' Ester asked.

'I'm not sure. I was hoping you could identify some specific mark, then at least we could be sure.'

Ester looked again at the ring. In her heart she knew it was hers but that was not the proof Adam needed.

'It isn't a crime to find something and pawn it,' he went on slowly. 'Assuming the ring was lost and not stolen anyone could have found it.

'They could also have handed it in to the police but, let's face it, many people would trade it in for cash.'

'Yes, but you've had problems with this woman before,' Ester reminded him.

'I have, but who's to say she has committed a crime? Even criminals fall on hard times.'

'I don't mean to be unkind but, if she'd fallen on hard times she could have pawned her own wedding ring,' Ester pointed out.

'Good point.' He looked at the ring again.

'Did you give her a fair price?'

'Of course!' he said, clearly taken aback at the question. 'I treated her as I would anyone else. I am not in a position to judge her circumstances.'

'I'm sorry,' Ester said quickly.

'Probably I should have sent her elsewhere,' he went on sadly, 'but then you wouldn't get your ring back.'

Ester wanted to tell him her ring meant nothing to her. Her husband hadn't been the man she thought she'd married.

He'd lied to her and spent her fortune, leaving them nothing. All the wedding ring meant was a means to obtain money to buy food and pay the rent.

She had a sudden thought and chose her words carefully.

'The woman in question, did you notice a very red patch on her arm where she might have suffered a nasty scald?'

Adam's expression said it all.

Ester sighed. The woman who'd found and pawned her wedding ring was none other than Norah Bagwell.

'Part of me feels sorry for her because she's had a hard life. But many of us have shown her friendship and kindness and we've lived to regret it.'

'Regret being kind?' Adam queried.

'No, I would probably do the same again. But on the last occasion I found her shivering and, as Ann was working at the Manor House and had lent me her lovely winter coat, I lent Norah my shawl.

'She knew it was only on loan and I'd need it back, but she went and pawned it!'

'Not here she didn't,' Adam replied.

'No, she went to the next village. It was cold and calculated and she treated others in the same way.

'I always say hello and give her a smile but I don't trust her any more.'

'So, where do we go from here?'

Ester shook her head.

'She was aware Edie had borrowed my ring and had lost it. The whole neighbourhood was out there looking for it — it's amazing Edie's husband didn't get wind of it.

'So Norah knew and didn't say a word when she found it.'

'Well, you had better have your ring back.' He held it out for Ester.

'I know it will mean extra paperwork for you, but may I exchange it for Edie's wedding ring?' Ester begged. 'At least, then, she can sleep easy.'

'She will still owe you for your ring,' he reminded her.

'I'm sure in time she'll pay me back, one way or another. Her needs are greater than mine just now.'

He nodded.

'In that case, take her ring and go and see her now.'

She thanked Adam, then frowned.

'If I do that, you become the loser. You gave Norah good money for my ring.

'By rights, you should keep it.'

Adam smiled.

'I appreciate the fact that you've realised that. I doubt anyone else will.

'But my needs are simple and I have no dependants, so do take it.

'Don't mention me when you return

it, though. I can't have people think I can give things away. That wouldn't be good for business at all!'

Unrest

It was a bad week not just for Tinker's Alley but also the surrounding area. Since raw materials were needed for the war effort they naturally took priority.

However this had a knock-on effect on the local factory where many of the women did a shift or two. Without the basic materials the factory couldn't carry on and had to close down.

That meant more people unemployed. The war had created a number of new jobs and some roles which were previously carried out by men were now being taken up by women but at a lower rate of pay.

The upshot was that less money was coming in but there were just as many mouths to feed.

Ester began to realise that the world was made up of two different sorts of people — those who counted their blessings, no matter how little they had, and those who moaned and complained regardless of whether they had a job or not.

There was a lot of unrest in the area. The men who, for whatever reason, had not gone away to fight were not happy about women being employed to do what they saw as men's jobs.

What would happen when the men came back, they asked, and no-one had the answer.

More and more employers were proving happy to take on women to do the work, especially as they could pay them less.

All this caused aggravation between the employers and the employed. Trade unions had a fine line to tread. They had to fight for what they believed was fair but, at the same time, they didn't want more people to lose their jobs.

One of the things that had always surprised Ester was how the poorest people often had a smile and a cheery word.

Nowadays there was now more poverty than ever and a smile was a rare sight.

Ester kept her head down and quietly went about her business, keeping herself to herself.

Life wasn't easy. Mrs Brown had fewer customers and so wasn't earning as much. This meant that she was cutting back on buying a new frock or having an old one altered.

Many women were pawning such basic items as bedding or even their undergarments, they were so desperate for money to buy food.

It didn't help that it was winter. Everyone was cold and hungry. There were few fruits or vegetables to be found nor berries or herbs growing to make a simple broth.

Ester had fewer reasons to visit the Emporium. People had either swallowed their pride and gone there themselves or simply had nothing left to pawn.

It troubled her to hear of fights in the street over a fallen potato left after the market traders had cleared away. She didn't want Polly to grow up witnessing such things.

From what she could tell, when she read yesterday's newspaper or listened to the news on the wireless when she was able to visit Adam, the news was not good and there was no sign that the war would end soon.

At night she curled up with a thin blanket on the floor and held her daughter. Their bodies kept each other warm.

Ester no longer had logs to burn in the grate.

More than once she lay awake wondering what she could do and how she could help others.

A Bright Idea

One morning Ester woke with an idea. It wouldn't solve everyone's problems but might make a difference to some. All she had to do was to speak to Adam and see what he thought.

She entered the dark pawnshop and waited a moment for her eyes to adjust.

'Good morning,' Adam said cheerfully. 'I haven't seen you or Polly for a while.'

'Good morning.'

Adam retrieved the box of playthings he kept for the child to amuse herself.

Polly ran to him to see if there was anything new to play with. She was becoming more confident the older she got.

'What can I do for you today?' Adam asked.

'I've an idea I want to discuss with you.'

'I'm all ears.' He folded his arms to show he was giving her his full attention.

'Your shop is crammed full of, well, things. Take that stuffed fox, for example, how long has that been there?'

'Probably since my father was a child!' Adam admitted. 'We'll have a ticket for it but it'll take me a while to find it.'

'I think we should take a stall in the market and see if we can sell some things.

'We can have a good look around and pick out a few useful, practical things like pots, pans and blankets, then add a few exotic things to attract people's attention.'

'And who will run this stall?' he asked.

'I hoped you would think it worth employing, maybe, two trusty people?'

'You have someone in mind?'

'I thought you might, but I could give it some thought if you want.'

Adam considered.

'Will anyone have money to buy my things? It's been very quiet for weeks.'

'I don't know but if you priced them low that would get things moving.' Ester suggested. 'It would help clear some of your stock and bring in money for you.

'It is no good owning a shop packed with so much you can't tell what you have.'

'You may have a point,' he agreed, 'I do know of two brothers I can trust, actually, and they have run a market stall in the past. I'll discuss it with them.

'Are you hoping to get commission on this?' he teased.

'All I want is to help,' she replied in dismay. 'Everyone is so miserable at the moment. I can't bear it any longer!'

Market Day

Monday, Wednesday and Friday were market days. That first Monday the brothers sold everything on the stall by lunchtime except a stuffed parrot and took back a tidy sum for Adam Boniface.

The same happened again on Wednesday. On Friday Adam asked if Ester could act as go-between.

If things were selling well she was to let Adam know. They would fill an old perambulator and she could push it down to the market to replenish stock.

'The only trouble is,' he admitted, 'I'm beginning to run out of useful, practical items. I've already let Robert know what we're doing in the hope he'd look out some of his old stock, but he now wants to give it a go himself!'

'Well, if he's going to employ people, that's not a bad thing,' Ester reminded him. 'I'm sure they'll be very grateful for the chance of work.'

On Friday she took Polly to the market. The weather was fine and it was busy.

Ester could see things were selling well and made her way to the Emporium to stock up.

On her way she thought about the people she saw there. It was a real mixture.

There were servants buying fresh fruit and vegetables for their mistresses alongside middle-class women browsing, having queued for meat at the butchers.

'I think you should include a wider range of goods,' Ester suggested when she reached the Emporium and told Adam about the different types of people she'd noticed shopping at the market.

She'd been hurrying so quickly she was quite out of breath. As she took a moment to recover she glanced around at the jumbled contents of the interior.

It never surprised her to spot something she hadn't noticed before.

'How long has that been there?' She pointed to a very pretty lady's hat. 'I think a few accessories like gloves and evening bags might be of interest.

'A vase or two, perhaps, some glassware, cigarette boxes, ash trays, snuffboxes . . . Nothing too valuable — it is a market, after all.'

As she talked Adam was dashing about collecting a hat here and a pair of mittens there, popping them in the perambulator for Ester to push back to the market.

It didn't take long for them to load it up but a few minutes' effort were needed to lift it down the steps.

'Are you sure you can manage?' he asked.

'I'm fine,' Ester replied cheerfully. 'Can you lift Polly up on the top, please?'

'I could,' Adam said, 'but it would be easier to steer without her. I don't suppose you'll be long, after all.'

Ester kneeled down to Polly's level and asked her what she wanted to do. Without a second thought Polly opted to stay and see what was in her playbox today.

'You spoil her,' Ester complained.

'I don't always put in something new in the box,' Adam was quick to reply. 'Only when I find something that I think will be of interest.'

'Thank you. I'm sure she'd be happy with a few building blocks and Bertie the bunny.'

★ ★ ★

Adam had been right — it didn't take Ester long to stock up the market stall. She left the perambulator with the brothers because they could then use it with their cart to transport any unsold goods at the end of the day.

'This looks different,' she said as soon as she entered the Emporium again.

Before her stood a hatstand bearing various hats and a host of walking-sticks and an umbrella at its base.

'You wouldn't believe it — it's been there all the time. It was hidden behind a mannequin wearing a uniform from the Boer War.

'Someone from the Garrick Theatre bought it last week. They're putting on comedy horror shows at the moment which are proving very popular.'

Ester made a face. She much preferred the simplicity of the moving pictures they'd watched recently.

While she loved to laugh and be entertained she had no wish to see anything horrible. Every day, in the newspapers and on the billboards, you could read about real-life horrid stories.

If she went to the theatre, she decided, she would want to be able to forget all the nasty things that were going on.

'I'm not complaining,' Adam continued. 'They also bought a Boer War rifle and even took the mannequin to play the role of a corpse!'

'I don't want to hear any more!' Ester laughed. 'I only want to hear nice things.'

With perfect timing they heard Polly singing quietly to Bertie as she rocked him to sleep. Ester's heart was filled with love for her daughter.

It amazed her that she had so little

in terms of material belongings and her life was undeniably hard at times, yet she could still feel both happy and content.

'Actually, I do have something nice to tell you,' Adam was saying.

Ester turned in his direction.

'Miss Clara came in with a cryptic message for you. I think I've got this right — she said she's found the shoes. Does that make any sense to you?'

Ester smiled and thought back to the conversation they'd had about the ancient wedding dress.

Quickly she rushed to the back of the shop, hoping it was still there.

'Adam, there was an old, white wedding dress right in the back of the shop. Miss Clara and I were looking at it.

'I can't see it; have you moved it, by any chance?'

'I suspect it was the one Miss Clara bought this afternoon. She asked if you would be able to call in at Moffat's and see her.'

'Of course. It must be for a customer

of hers,' Ester said, relieved. 'I wonder if she wants me to make any alterations to it.'

The Landlord's Visit

Ester and her neighbours usually paid her rent to the rent collector but on this occasion the landlord himself decided to come and collect what was owed.

Several tenants took the opportunity of complaining to him about damp or broken windows, chimneys in need of cleaning or doors that didn't close properly.

By the time he knocked on Ester's door he wasn't in a good mood. He spotted her sewing-machine and told her she was only paying him rent for living accommodation. It would cost extra to use the premises to carry on her work.

'I'm sorry, I wasn't aware of that,' Ester said quietly. Inside she was fuming because it made no difference what she did in her dreary single room. 'I don't know if I can afford to pay you more.'

'In that case you'd better move that machine by the time the next rent's due. Don't think my rent collector won't notice. I'll make sure he checks up on you.'

Ester sighed. It was so unfair! She needed to work to earn money to pay the rent.

Why did the man have to make it so difficult for her to make ends meet?

She had a week to solve the problem.

'Hide it,' one neighbour suggested. 'We'll tip you off when the rent collector's coming and you can slip it out the back. He'll never know.'

'But that's dishonest!' Ester cried.

The look on the woman's face told her that was why she would never really fit in with this sort of life.

Ester was brought up to be honourable. Her neighbour had been brought up to survive these awful conditions.

'I'll find a way round it,' Ester told her, 'But thank you for your help.'

'He only said he'd charge you extra because he knows you will pay,' the woman added.

Ester nodded. That was probably true. She always paid her rent in full and on time, hating the thought of being in arrears and owing money.

She lived in fear of being evicted and thrown out on the street or, even worse, to end up taking Polly to the workhouse.

That evening she finished off the alterations to the wedding dress.

It had been a surprise to her to learn that Miss Clara was engaged to be married! Her young man was a poorly paid rector and she couldn't afford a gown from Moffat's.

Besides, she'd fallen in love with the dress at the Emporium and, now that Ester had altered it, it fitted her perfectly and with minimum expense.

Ester returned the dress just as Miss Clara was shutting up shop. They could use the long looking-glass without being disturbed.

'I have a favour to ask,' Ester told her. 'I've done several alterations for your customers now and wonder if it would be possible to keep my machine in a tiny corner here.'

She explained about her landlord

charging her extra rent for working at home.

'I will mention it to Mrs Brown, the owner. I know you've done work for her so she might be agreeable,' the girl said.

The news that Moffat's was owned by Mrs Brown came as a surprise to Ester.

'The only problem,' Miss Clara went on, 'is that when I marry Reverend Stevens I shall leave here and live at the rectory. My job then will be to help him in parish work.

'I don't know who is going to take over from me here.'

'I would still like you to ask Mrs Brown on my behalf, please,' Ester begged.

★ ★ ★

On her way home, carrying a sleeping Polly, Ester thought about what Clara had said.

She remembered the dream she had had about having her own dress shop where she could offer alterations.

Perhaps the best thing to do would be

to go and speak to Mrs Brown herself?

The more she thought about it the more sense it made.

Instead of Ester earning a little here from repairs and a penny there for mending, or from commission on something sold at the Emporium that she had reworked, working at Moffat's would mean regular income for her.

The only problem would be Polly. Ester would have to find someone to care for her and that would cost money.

Suddenly she thought of Adam's Aunt Maud and wondered if they could come to some sort of arrangement.

That would be the ideal solution. Perhaps things were beginning to look up, after all.

By the time Ester arrived home she had made up her mind to approach Mrs Brown and to speak with Aunt Maud.

She pushed open the door. The room was dark but, even before she had lit a candle, she sensed something was wrong.

The table was bare. Her treasured Singer sewing-machine was missing!

High Hopes

Ester contacted Constable Harris but he didn't seem interested. She felt he still saw her as a criminal, despite having been exonerated after Ann's husband admitted he'd given her the locket.

Constable Harris questioned her about how she came to have the luxury of a sewing-machine in the first place, rather than offering to search for the culprit.

In need of a friend, she went to call on Adam. The lights were out in the shop and, although she tapped on the door, no-one came to see who it was.

Feeling quite alone she made her way home, doing her best to sound cheerful for Polly's sake.

Fortunately the child had fallen asleep again and, although she was a heavy weight to carry, at least she had not heard the conversation with Constable Harris.

Eventually they reached the cold, dark room they called home. Carefully laying

Polly down Ester fumbled around in the dark to find a candle and her tinderbox.

No sooner had she lit up the room when her neighbour appeared, looking furtive.

'Shall I bring it back now?'

'What?' Ester was tired and miserable.

'That machine of yours,' the woman said. 'Shall I bring it back?'

'You have it?' Ester couldn't believe it. 'Why did you take it?'

'You never know when that rent man will come snooping. I thought it best to get it out of sight.'

'I wish you'd told me what you were going to do,' Ester said, trying to keep her voice even.

She understood the woman had been trying to help. She wasn't keen on the thought of her coming and going in and out of her home while Ester was out, but such was the way they lived.

'Yes, please,' she told her. 'There's no need to do it again. I think I've found somewhere to keep it from now on.'

The woman duly returned it and

clearly wanted to be paid for her assistance but Ester explained she had nothing to give her.

The following morning Ester took more care than usual with her appearance and went to pay Aunt Maud a visit at her home.

It brought back happy memories of the night Adam took her to the Picture Palace and they all had tea with Aunt Maud and Cousin Robert and his wife.

To her dismay she found the house locked up and no signs of life.

Her plan was proving more difficult than she'd hoped. She certainly didn't want to trouble Adam Boniface but she needed to see Mrs Brown as a matter of urgency and taking Polly with her wasn't a good idea.

'I'm really sorry to bother you,' Ester told Adam at the Emporium.

He was in the process of moving things about and didn't seem to be listening.

'I need to ask you a favour. It's important, otherwise I wouldn't ask.'

'Does it have to be now?' he asked, not

unkindly. He was trying to manoeuvre a chest of drawers.

Just at that moment, Aunt Maud appeared like a fairy godmother in a fairytale. She must have seen Ester's face drop.

'Would you like me to mind Polly for a little while?' she offered.

'Oh! I can see why you're Adam's favourite aunt,' Ester said, relieved. 'I'm going to see Mrs Brown about a job and I don't think I ought to take Polly with me.'

'A job?' Aunt Maud asked.

'I'll tell you all about it when I get back,' Ester promised. 'I shouldn't be more than an hour. I'll hurry straight back.'

She kissed Polly on the forehead and practically ran out of the door.

Begging

Mrs Brown greeted her in a friendly manner. They discussed the work she had done for her and for customers at Moffat's.

'I understand from Miss Clara that you are looking for someone to take over from her. I would like to put myself forward.'

'I am aware of your skills and also your circumstances but the post has already been filled,' the older woman replied.

'Oh.' Ester couldn't help but voice her disappointment.

'If it's a job you want I hear women are being recruited to drive ambulances and buses. If you can't drive they offer training.'

'Thank you. I'd foolishly set my heart on your dress shop. I thought being able to offer a bespoke service might work well.'

'I'm sure something will come up,' Mrs Brown said, dismissing Ester.

As she reached the door she paused and glanced back at Mrs Brown, feeling compelled to ask.

'I'm not sure if Miss Clara mentioned my idea of converting a corner of your dress shop for my machine so we could offer alterations on the premises?'

'She did mention it.' Mrs Brown nodded. 'I'd rather use the space to display examples of dresses we could make for the discerning lady about town!'

'Could I not be the one to make those dresses?' Ester asked, aware that she was practically begging for the work.

'I'm fully staffed at the moment. As I say, I'm aware of your skills and in future I may call upon you. But I have no work for you at present. Understand?'

Ester nodded and left with her head down, making her way back to the Emporium.

As she passed through the market square she bumped into her old friend, Ann.

'How lovely to see you! Have things worked out as you hoped?'

'They certainly have, although we now have a group of young lasses to work the land. As soon as I've learned something I'm teaching these young girls what to do!

'Still, we have a laugh and it's nice to have some company.'

'What about Bobby and Mary?'

'Bobby's grown another six inches! He's almost as tall as me and strong as an ox.

'He's very useful around the farm and Mary's proving helpful. And your Polly?'

At that moment, the children caught sight of their mother and rushed over. They'd been looking at a nearby market stall.

'My, you have grown!' Ester said to Bobby who stood tall and proud in his Boy Scout uniform.

Mary was dressed as a Girl Guide although Ester wondered if she was old enough.

'What have you been doing?'

'I'm learning first aid,' Mary said proudly. 'I can bandage your leg and put your arm in a sling.'

'That's very good. And don't you both look smart in your uniforms!'

'How's Polly?' Mary asked as she looked around for her small friend.

'She's fine. I've got to go and fetch her,' Ester said. 'Lovely to see you all.'

Ester rushed off again but slowed down as the Emporium came in sight. She had been so confident Mrs Brown would welcome her into her employment.

Now she had no good news to tell.

She had briefly considered what she could do for the war effort but driving ambulances was not for her.

She knew she needed to be able to do something where she could continue to keep one eye on Polly.

Mrs Brown had said that something would come up. Ester hoped that was true.

All Change

To Ester's surprise there was a hive of activity when she entered the shop. Even Polly was carrying things back and forth.

'What's going on?' she asked as she took off her shawls. 'Can I help?'

'I've had a bit of a tumble and I've hurt my hip,' Aunt Maud said, waving the walking-stick that Ester realised she'd seen her use earlier.

Ester had been so focused on visiting Mrs Brown that she had not questioned Aunt Maud. Now she felt awful that she had burdened her with an active two-year-old!

'I'm so sorry! I should have noticed.'

'Polly's been a delight, as usual,' Aunt Maud was quick to say. 'I had been feeling sorry for myself but she sang me a song and has cheered me up no end.'

Ester smiled.

'So, what is happening?' she repeated.

'I've too many steps and stairs at home and things were going from bad to worse.

But Adam has come up with a solution.

'He's very generously said I can have his room and kitchenette down here behind the counter and he's going to move upstairs to his stock room.'

'I didn't know he had a stock room!'

Ester laughed as Polly toddled by, carefully carrying three books. She placed them down and immediately turned round to go and fetch more.

'I shan't say, but I thought the shop looked better because he'd shifted a bit of stock lately. Now he's filled it up again!'

'At least it looks different and his regulars may notice something new to buy.'

Ester found Adam and helped move stock from the room upstairs down into the shop.

'Shall I take this?' she asked, referring to a box of china in the corner.

'I'm not emptying the whole room,' Adam explained. 'I just need to clear enough space for my few bits and pieces.

'I thought that china might be good to try and sell on the market stall?'

Ester nodded in agreement and looked at the room. If he used the entire room to live in it would be a fair size. At least the sun shone through the windows, even on a cold winter's day.

She understood why he'd decided only to use a small area. Hopefully, in time, he could move the rest of the stock downstairs and ultimately sell it on.

'Right,' he said. 'Now I need to move my things up here.'

Ester watched as he collected together his possessions. He had a few books, bedding, wash jug and bowl and some family photos.

She carried these while he took up a small fireside chair and then came down for a cabinet.

A thin wooden bed and walnut wardrobe were already upstairs so he would make use of these. Ester arranged his spare trousers and Sunday-best suit on hangers.

They'd just finished when the two market boys arrived with a cart containing the most useful of Aunt Maud's things.

'Is there more to come?'

Ester remembered visiting her home and recalled a piano, glass cabinets of collectables, numerous photographs and paintings on the walls.

She had enough chairs for them all to sit and take tea. There was a pretty cake stand made from cherry wood, occasional tables, a clock on the mantelpiece and a musical box which had amused Polly.

'No. I've brought my sewing-box and some knitting. I'm making socks for the war effort! This is my fourth pair but I've run out of pullovers to unravel.'

It seemed the house itself was to be locked up, at least for the time being.

As the daylight faded they sat down. They were dusty and tired but Aunt Maud had her new 'home', Adam was installed upstairs and everything was in order.

'I'm made soup and there's a loaf of bread. Will you and Polly join us?' Aunt Maud asked. 'You've earned it.'

Ester was about to decline, knowing

how scarce food was for everyone, but Aunt Maud wouldn't take no for an answer.

To be honest, Ester had no wish to return to her lonely room with no-one to talk to apart from her shadow once Polly was asleep.

'Sit down,' Ester urged. 'I can stir it and serve it up.'

'I don't mind if I do.'

Aunt Maud eased herself into her chair and straight away Polly came and sat next to her.

'I think this arrangement will work very well,' she predicted. 'I can cook for Adam and he can keep an eye on me.

'It will be company for us both.'

Ester nodded. She didn't dare turn around to face Aunt Maud for fear of her revealing her true feelings.

Never before today had she felt quite so alone.

Contentment

Adam bolted the doors and pulled down the blinds before coming to join them in what was now Aunt Maud's sitting-room. He arranged four chairs around a small dining-room table.

Aunt Maud handed Ester a tablecloth.

'We ought to do this properly as it's our first meal here!' She smiled. 'Adam, I am so grateful for your generosity. How can I thank you for taking in an old woman?'

'You're not just any old woman! You're my favourite aunt, remember?'

'Are you Robert's mother?' Ester asked as she tried to work out the family connections.

'No, actually I'm no relation at all. I was a great friend of Adam's mother — we were like sisters. In truth, Adam has had several aunts and uncles and so I feel very touched to be called his favourite.'

They ate their bread and soup whilst chatting. Once again Ester was filled with contentment.

Adam and his aunt made her feel as though she and Polly were an important part of their little family, yet none of them were related.

Once Ester had cleared away the meal she told Polly it was time to go.

'Bertie?' Polly cried.

Everyone looked around for the toy rabbit. He was not in any of the usual places where Polly played, but then so many things had been moved around that day.

They began to look under things and behind boxes but he was nowhere to be found.

Polly began to shed a few tears and suck her thumb for comfort.

Adam picked her up and said he had something special to show her. He reached under his desk and hidden away he found a copy of another Beatrix Potter book.

This one was 'The Tale Of The Flopsy Bunnies'.

Adam read the story and showed her the pictures, leaving Aunt Maud and

Ester to talk quietly.

'Forgive me,' Aunt Maud said. 'I'd forgotten to ask you how your meeting with Mrs Brown had gone.'

Ester's expression must have given away how she felt.

'Never mind.' Aunt Maud reached out and squeezed Ester's hand. 'Maybe it wasn't meant to be.'

Factory Girls

Everyone was encouraged to 'do their bit' for the country in these times. Children collected conkers so that chemicals could be extracted to make bullets and shells.

Older children took messages and collected blankets, books and knitted garments, all to be sent to the soldiers fighting abroad.

Ester managed to get a job in a factory making uniforms. The material was thick and it was hard work on the fingers but the other girls in the machine room were friendly and they were all in the same boat.

They all had families to care for, food to prepare and rent to pay as well as working to earn a living.

On one of the breaks Ester listened to a couple of ladies discussing how they were going to set up a Women's Institute group. Someone was going to visit them and show them what had to be done.

'What sort of group is it?' one lady asked.

Ester was eager to hear the reply because, although she'd read in the paper about the Women's Institute, she didn't really know much about it.

'The idea is for a group of women to get together. Everyone is welcome, whether you're rich or poor,' one of the women said. 'Then we have a speaker — either someone to entertain us or to teach us a new skill.

'After that we have tea and cake, where we can chat to each other and make new friends.'

'It sounds great but how could I get a night out?' one woman, Alice, asked.

'Can't your old man look after the kids just one night a month?'

There was a roar of laughter at this. The woman decided she would start dropping hints now and, by the time they'd set up a meeting, he might have got used to the thought of it.

'How about you, Ester?' one of the girls asked. 'Will you come along?'

'I'm a widow. I don't have any family to look after my daughter,' Ester told them.

'Who has her right now?'

'A friend of a friend and I already feel very much in her debt. It's one thing to ask if I'm working and doing my bit.

'I couldn't ask her to have Polly just so I could have a night off!'

The first woman nodded.

'Maybe things will be different by the time we're organised.'

'I hope so. Or perhaps you can just tell me what happened and what you learned,' Ester suggested.

'I could but I think you'd be missing out. A big part of the Women's Institute is meeting people and making friends.

'Leave it with me and I'll see what I can do,' Alice went on. 'There must be some way around it. You're not the only woman bringing up a family on her own at the moment!'

★ ★ ★

191

Ester found she did well at the factory, mainly because she was already familiar with a sewing-machine and with making garments.

She was also a quick learner and, in no time, she found herself in charge of a group of much younger girls who had not worked much since leaving school.

As the girls were so young and inexperienced Ester often found herself acting in the role of parent.

She listened to their problems, which usually involved a similarly young sweetheart about to go off to war.

As much as she found she enjoyed the work and had already grown fond of 'her' girls, she realised she had a tendency to dwell on their problems when, really, she had enough of her own.

There were two main issues. The first was that, despite working all hours, she was unable to save very much.

Without any money behind her she knew she could never improve her chances of getting on in the world.

It wasn't that she was unhappy in the

life that she was now living. In fact, she often felt more contented than ever.

What concerned her was that everything was still a struggle and that she had very little to show for her labours.

The second thing was that she missed Polly dreadfully and longed to have more time with her. Every day the little girl seemed to learn a new word or master a nursery rhyme.

Polly herself seemed to have adapted well to her new life of spending more and more time with Aunt Maud and less time with her mother.

Ester did what she could to help Aunt Maud. She did chores in order to repay her, but continued to feel in her debt.

Emergency!

By the end of the week Ester's troubles had been on her mind so much that she decided to stay late and speak with her supervisor.

The woman was an older lady and Ester admired her wisdom and fair decisions.

They had just begun talking in the upstairs office when they heard a crash followed by a scream. They rushed to the workshop. The factory workers had already left, no doubt looking forward to their weekend.

By the time Ester reached the shop floor it was in darkness. She lit a gas light. Its yellowy glow gave the room an eerie feel.

A cabinet had toppled over, shunting along a table which, in turn, had dislodged a pile of storage boxes. Someone, it seemed, was trapped underneath.

Together the women righted the furniture that had fallen. It took all their strength to lift a heavy cabinet out of the way, ensuring they kept the doors shut so the contents didn't spill out and make matters worse.

Eventually they found two victims who had been crushed beneath. One woman lay very still but Ester could see the other lady was still breathing.

'I'll get help!' the supervisor said and rushed from the room.

Ester leaned closer and spoke quietly and calmly to the injured woman.

'It's Ester. Don't worry, help is on its way. Can you speak? Does anything hurt?'

The woman gave a little cough which clearly hurt her chest. Ester could tell she was having trouble breathing.

'I'll get you some water,' Ester suggested and made to move.

'Stay,' the woman whispered. 'Don't leave me.'

Ester stayed with her, stroking her brow and holding her hand. Every so often she looked to see if the supervisor was back. She seemed to be taking for ever.

Ester wished she knew what to do. Instinctively she kept the woman calm, reassured her she would be all right and checked to make sure nothing else was likely to fall on them.

A piece of fabric was draped over the nearest machine. Ester pulled it towards them and used it as a blanket to help keep the woman warm.

After what seemed an incredibly long time the supervisor returned, followed closely by two women in white uniforms each bearing a red cross.

They checked both the victims and assessed the situation.

'What happened?' one asked.

'I'm not sure,' Ester began. 'We were in an office upstairs and heard a crash. It must have been some furniture falling over.

'I don't know why they were here. Everyone should have gone home. These two must have come back for something.'

'There's a stretcher in the back of the van. Can you fetch it?'

Ester and her supervisor made a

dash for the van and carried in the first stretcher.

Expertly and gently the British Red Cross volunteers lifted the woman on to the stretcher and took her to the vehicle.

'Help me,' one of them said to Ester as she gestured to another stretcher.

They carried it back in and, with the same tender care, lifted the other body on to it and took it to the van.

The nurses sat in the back as Ester's supervisor took the wheel of the van.

She threw a set of keys at Ester.

'Lock up for me!' she called. 'We'll talk again on Monday.'

Ester watched as the van roared off. Silently she prayed for the woman and the volunteers.

A Comfort

'What's wrong?' Aunt Maud asked when she set eyes on Ester later that evening.

'There was an accident.' Ester looked from Aunt Maud to Polly and back again.

'Come in and sit down.' Aunt Maud hobbled to the kitchen using her stick. 'Polly, go and fetch Mr Boniface, please, quickly now.'

The child returned a moment later dragging Adam by the hand. Instantly he opened his arms to draw Ester in.

The only other time he had cradled her in his arms was when she had been in a prison cell, wrongly accused of theft.

Until now Ester had managed to keep her emotions in check, but the feeling of Adam's strong arms around her made her relax and the tears began as she tried to explain what had happened.

'Polly, go and help Auntie in the kitchen,' Adam said. 'What happened?' he asked Ester as he gently stroked her back.

Polly 'helped' Aunt Maud push in a small tea trolley bearing a tray of tea. Aunt Maud passed around cups and saucers while Polly tried to climb on the bottom of the trolley.

It was while she was doing this that she noticed a little white paw.

'Bertie!' She pulled at the paw until the much-loved rabbit was found and hugged.

The hot, sweet tea had revived Ester and she explained what had happened.

'How is the woman now?'

'I don't know.' Ester shook her head. 'I'm not sure which hospital they were going to or how seriously she was injured.

'I just didn't know what to do!'

Ester sobbed and Adam put his arm protectively around her.

'I'm sure you being there must have been a huge comfort to the poor soul.'

'I kept thinking, what would my father have done?' Ester told them. 'He'd have known the right thing to do.'

'He was a trained doctor. I'm sure you did all the right things.'

'I did cover her with a makeshift blanket,' Ester said. 'I offered to get her water but she didn't want me to leave her. I do hope she's going to be all right.'

The long day and shock of the accident had exhausted her and she soon fell asleep in the chair.

Adam covered her with a blanket and made a little nest for Polly before returning upstairs to his own quarters.

Keeping Your Head

Ester woke to the sound of the kettle whistling and the smell of toast.

'How are you this morning?' Aunt Maud asked. 'You look brighter than last night.'

'I'm sorry!' Ester accepted a cup of tea. 'I was in a state. It won't happen again.'

'Don't be silly. You'd had a shock. It's a credit to you that you did what you could.'

'I was just upset because I was so ill-prepared. I should have known what to do.

'I'm a doctor's daughter! I'm used to dealing with sick patients.'

'Don't be too hard on yourself.' Adam appeared in the doorway. 'I've been thinking — they'll have taken the injured women to the nearest hospital.

'Once we close this afternoon we could go and make enquiries. You'd feel better if you knew how she was doing.'

'I would,' Ester agreed as she poured Adam a cup of tea. 'Thank you.'

'Adam, would it help if I manned the shop this afternoon?' Aunt Maud offered. 'Saturday afternoons are never very busy, are they?

'Besides, it looks as though it's going to keep raining all day so that should keep customers at home.'

'Thank you, Aunt Maud. That would be helpful, then we can go in daylight,' Adam declared and so it was decided.

Even several hours later the rain was still pouring and the streets were awash with puddles.

Adam had found an old raincoat for Ester to wear. It had obviously belonged to a young boy or a small man but despite this, it was still too big. However, it did a good job of keeping off some of the rain.

At the hospital they managed to track down the injured woman. This was little short of a miracle as they didn't even know her name.

Fortunately it had been logged that there had been an accident at the factory and that two women had been admitted.

Adam held back as Ester rushed over to see the woman who was now lying on crisp, white sheets in a hospital bed.

'Thank goodness you're all right!' Ester told her. 'I've been so worried about you.'

The patient gave a weak smile, squeezed Ester's hand and drifted back off to sleep.

'She needs rest,' one of the Red Cross nurses told her. 'You did a good job yesterday.'

'Did I?' Ester looked up in surprise. 'I felt so useless.'

'Yes. You kept her conscious and warm. You reassured her and stayed with her, bringing her comfort.'

Ester moved away from the bed and whispered to the nurse.

'Will she make a good recovery?'

'Physically she's just bruised and suffering from shock. We haven't yet told her about her companion. That's when she will need a friend, sadly.'

'Does she have any relatives I ought to

visit?' Ester asked.

'I think your supervisor did that last night. She spoke with both families.'

Ester sat with the woman, stroking her hand, for a little while and then promised she'd visit her again.

'May I have a word?' one of the nurses asked as Ester was leaving with Adam by her side. 'You do know we're always after volunteers?

'You've got a good bedside manner and yesterday it was reported that you kept your head. The last thing we need, you see, is a volunteer who goes to pieces.'

Ester thought about the tears she'd shed the previous night. However she had kept her emotions at bay when it mattered.

'I know the Girl Guides are being taught about first aid,' Ester replied. 'I'm responsible for a group of young ladies at the factory. I think we all ought to learn the basics of first aid.

'Then, if anything like this were to happen again, at least we'd know what to do.'

The nurse nodded.

'We're giving a talk in the town hall on Thursday at six. It would be great if you could bring along as many people as you can.'

Ester looked up at Adam.

'Don't worry,' he told her. 'I'm sure Polly will be happy with Aunt Maud, especially now she's found Bertie again!'

'Just one more thing,' the nurse asked. 'I shall need a volunteer to be bandaged on Thursday. Can I count on you?'

'That's the least I can do!' Ester laughed. 'Although I'd really like a chance to learn how to do it myself.'

'Don't worry about that,' the nurse assured her. 'Once we've shown everyone what to do there will be plenty of opportunity to have a practice.'

'In that case,' Ester said gaily, 'I'll see you on Thursday!'

A War On

Early on Monday morning Ester went in to work. She still had the keys and was keen to see her supervisor and help her make sure the area was safe before they allowed anyone in to the workshop.

'I don't know what I'd have done without you on Friday,' her supervisor told her. 'We made a good team.'

Ester confided that she'd visited the surviving girl in hospital and had spent some time on Sunday making a couple of posters advertising the first-aid course at the town hall at six on Thursday.

'I see I'll have to keep my wits about me,' the supervisor joked, 'or you'll be after my job!'

'Actually,' Ester said with a grin, 'that's what I'd been wanting to talk to you about on Friday before all this happened.'

'What? My job?'

'No. Mine.'

'I'll walk with you to the Emporium to

fetch your little girl with you after work this evening,' the supervisor offered. 'We can talk then.'

The day went slowly. Everyone was in a sombre mood since the accident.

Eventually, the bell rang and they were free to go. Ester looked around for her supervisor.

'Oh, yes,' the woman said, 'you wanted a quick word.'

Ester's heart sank. She wasn't after a short chat — she wanted time to be able to explain her situation in full to this woman, to ask for her advice.

Instead, she could only explain briefly that she was finding it hard relying on friends to care for Polly while she worked.

She did manage to hint that one day she would want more from a job and that she felt she was capable of taking on more responsibility if the role was the right one.

'Mrs Sharp, there's a war on and everyone has to do their bit. We're all finding it hard. There's nothing any of us can do about it so it's no use complaining.'

The supervisor gave a sigh.

'You could always have her evacuated. That would free you up.'

'She's too young,' Ester replied quickly. 'Polly's only two. I'd have to go with her and that won't solve the problem.'

'Lie about her age. You wouldn't be the first,' the supervisor suggested in all seriousness. 'You're slight; that would explain why she's small for her age.'

'I can't do that!' Ester was horrified at the thought of being parted from Polly and she certainly wasn't comfortable about lying to the authorities.

'Can I reduce my hours at all?' Ester asked, frustrated by the situation.

'Certainly not. We have new recruits I need you to train up. You're doing a good job with the young girls.

'Well done for keeping up morale today. It's not an easy time. See you tomorrow.'

Ester was cross. It hadn't gone as well as she'd hoped.

She pulled her coat closer around her. The temperature had dropped and she shivered as she hurried through the market place on her way to the Emporium to collect Polly.

The brothers who ran the market stall had been doing a fine job. They had managed to sell quite a bit of bric-à-brac as well as a few more fancy goods.

The box of china that had sat upstairs in Adam's room had been sold, as well as various small items such as hats, walking-canes, gloves and cooking pots.

'They even sold a couple of Toby jugs! At a good price, too,' Adam told her.

'It is looking better in here,' she said approvingly. 'It feels more organised.

'I like the way you've grouped things, too. It's so much easier to find things.'

'I quite liked the way it was,' Adam admitted. 'As a child I always loved finding something you weren't expecting. Like sheets of music in a coal scuttle or a snuffbox in a bowler hat!'

That evening, when Ester had arrived to collect Polly, she had noticed Aunt Maud grimace a couple of times as she moved about.

She shared her concerns with Adam when he came to say goodbye as Ester was taking Polly home.

He nodded. There was no need to say more.

'I have spoken with my supervisor at work but I can't change my hours,' she told him. 'I'm needed to train up the new recruits, apparently. At least she knows how I feel.'

'Don't worry about the first-aid course on Thursday,' Adam assured her. 'I'll give Aunt Maud a hand with Polly until you come back.'

'I really don't know what I'd do without you — and your aunt,' Ester added and felt herself blush. 'You've been a real friend to us both.'

She kissed Polly on the cheek and gave Adam a smile.

First Aid

Ester felt guilty leaving Polly for longer but Aunt Maud and Adam had both reassured her that they loved having her and had plans for a special evening.

As much as she was looking forward to learning first aid she was torn. A large part of her wanted to be warm and cosy in the Emporium with Polly, Aunt Maud and Adam. Her new 'family'.

She reminded herself that, if she wasn't doing the course, then there would be no reason for Polly to remain at the pawnshop and the two of them would be huddling together in their dark and dingy room.

Ester was greeted by the nurse from the hospital. Because she had agreed to be a 'patient' she was ushered off to a side room and given a welcome cup of tea.

The evening was well organised and turned out to be terrific fun.

The nurse had made it look so easy

to put Ester's arm in a sling but later, when they were all paired up and had a go themselves, there was a great deal of laughter. It wasn't as easy as it looked!

This broke the ice and, after the girls were given a cup of tea and a biscuit, they all paid more careful attention when it came to assessing a situation and looking for signs of life; for example, after an air raid.

It turned out to be a very jolly evening and by the end of it all the girls were eager to sign up to be 'on call' should an emergency occur.

At least, now, they felt they would be able to hold the fort until trained medical staff arrived.

'Excuse me, do you have a moment?' a well-spoken doctor asked Ester as she was reaching for her coat.

'Certainly. How can I help?'

'It's a personal matter.' He steered her to a quiet corner of the room. 'You have impressed me this evening. I liked the way you encouraged and praised the other girls.

'I could tell you have some medical knowledge, too. Are you in training?'

'My father was a doctor, a general practitioner. I used to help him whenever I could. I suppose I picked up some things.'

Ester frowned.

'At one time I considered training to be a doctor like my father. It wasn't meant to be and my life has taken a different direction.'

'Are you happy?' he surprised her by asking.

She had already noticed how he looked at her hands and, no doubt, had noticed the absence of a wedding ring.

'I'm not unhappy,' she began, choosing her words with care. 'I am a widow with a young daughter.'

'I rely on the kindness of others which is hard because I don't like being in their debt, but I can't repay them at the moment.'

'That's very worthy of you,' he replied.

The nursing staff who'd been on duty were folding up bandages and packing things away as they chatted happily amongst themselves.

'I have a proposition,' the doctor said. 'I have an elderly father who used to be a GP like your father. He's a wealthy man and has all his faculties, but he's no longer very mobile and can't look after himself.

'That makes him, well, irritable. I admit housekeepers haven't tended to stay long, but I feel you're made of stronger stuff.'

'As I say, I have a daughter,' Ester said. 'She's only two and can be demanding.'

She hoped he, too, wouldn't suggest she lie about Polly's age and have her evacuated from the city.

'My father's speciality was paediatrics. He's always telling me to find a good woman and provide him with a brood of grandchildren!' The doctor laughed. 'At least give it some thought.'

'I'm not sure . . .' Ester began.

But the doctor was already writing out his name and telephone number.

'If you're serious about going into

214

medicine I know my father would be delighted to teach you a thing or two — in fact he'd relish it!

'It would do him good. Everyone needs to feel useful and, as I say, there's nothing wrong with his mind.'

'But I told you I'm not unhappy with my current arrangements,' Ester protested.

'I detect you are not entirely happy, though. Am I correct?'

Ester nodded. He had summed up her situation accurately.

'I can arrange for you to meet my father. He's a generous man. You could bring your little girl with you, if you like.

'You'd have to live in but it's a family house — very comfortable with plenty of room and a decent-sized garden.

'I think you could be very happy there.'

'I appreciate your offer, but . . .'

'Sleep on it,' he interrupted and thrust his details into her hand. 'It's been a pleasure to meet you, Mrs Sharp. I do hope you will think seriously about my offer.'

Mixed Feelings

Polly was sound asleep in a little bed which had been made up in the corner of Aunt Maud's room.

She was clutching Bertie and other toys lay in a little cardboard box beside her. On the wall was a picture she had drawn.

Ester felt a pang of envy. She would have liked to be able to give Polly such things.

Until now she had comforted herself by reminding herself that Polly knew she was loved and cherished. That counted a great deal. Sadly, not every child could feel that.

'You're quiet,' Aunt Maud said. 'How did the course go? Was it useful?'

Adam had insisted she warm herself by the fire. He gave her a hot cup of black tea. Polly had drunk their ration of milk.

'The course was excellent. I thoroughly enjoyed it and so did all the other girls.'

'But?' Aunt Maud asked perceptively.

'At the end of the evening one doctor asked if I would consider caring for his elderly father. It would be a live-in role and I could take Polly with me.'

'I see.' Aunt Maud looked up at Adam who stood in the alcove which separated the kitchen from the living quarters.

Ester looked up at him, too.

'I'm not unhappy,' she said quickly, 'but I feel so very much in your debt. I wish I could repay you in some way.'

'Speaking for myself,' Aunt Maud said, 'I love having Polly. You owe me nothing as I feel I'm doing my bit by enabling you to work making uniforms for our soldiers.

'We all have to pull together.'

'Besides, you share your rations and more than once you've cooked us a meal,' Adam added. 'Tell us more about this offer.'

He sat down beside them. They spoke quietly so as not to disturb Polly.

'The old gentleman was a doctor himself. His son thinks he might teach me some medical things. Just the basics, but . . .'

'You told me before that you wanted to become a doctor like your father.' Adam nodded his understanding.

'I admit it is tempting, even if I discover it isn't really what I want.'

'I, too, have a confession,' Adam began.

Ester's heart did a flip as she wondered what he was going to say.

'I have never been happy about you living in that horrid little room. It's damp and Polly used to cough a lot.

'I think she has improved by spending her days here. I'd be much happier if you were living somewhere which would be warmer and more comfortable.'

Although she was touched that he had been concerned about her living conditions he wasn't offering her a home.

The thought struck her like a thunderbolt — somehow she'd fallen in love with Adam Boniface without noticing it.

In the next moment she realised that he didn't have the same feelings for her. Thank goodness she hadn't embarrassed herself by making any assumptions.

'Would you actually be earning money or just be given board and lodging?' Aunt Maud wanted to know. 'I'm only thinking about your ability to save.

'I know you are desirous of improving your lot.'

'I'm not entirely sure,' Ester confessed. 'The doctor did say his father was generous. It's something I'd have to ask about.'

'My father was also a doctor,' Aunt Maud told her.

Ester was surprised — she had never said this before.

'I never saw myself following in his footsteps but I have always been interested in medicine and I do read medical papers.'

'Really?'

'Yes. From now on, I shall pass them on to you. It will ensure that you continue to visit us. That way we'll see Polly, too.'

'Of course we would visit you! Do you think I should take him up on his offer, then?' Ester asked anxiously.

'I do. I've been reading recently about Doctor Louisa Aldrich-Blake. Quite an amazing woman.

'There ought to be more lady doctors and you would make a good one, Ester.'

Ester wasn't as confident in herself as Maud was. But she'd never know if she didn't take this opportunity.

'What do you think?' she said, looking directly at Adam.

He had such lovely grey eyes. In the flicker of the firelight, however, they looked sad.

'As I said, it will give you the opportunity to provide better living conditions for yourself and Polly. That's important.'

He hesitated and, once again, Ester realised she was holding her breath.

'Go and meet this man first to make sure you know what you're letting yourself in for.'

Ester nodded.

She knew these two people had her best interests at heart but she was going to miss them.

A New Position

Young Dr Bentley was delighted to hear her decision and immediately arranged for Ester to meet with his father.

'I'll take you there myself. Tell me what time you finish work and I'll pick you up in my motor car.'

Ester couldn't help smiling to herself. It would cause quite a stir if young, handsome Dr Bentley arrived in his car to collect her from work.

'I'll walk over to the hospital and meet you there,' Ester suggested instead.

If nothing came of her visit no-one would be any the wiser. It was better that way.

Once they were en route Ester realised Dr Bentley Senior lived just the other side of the Emporium in a smart part of town.

'My daughter is being cared for by the aunt of the pawnbroker. Would it be possible to stop there first so I can collect Polly and bring her along, too?'

The doctor took out his pocket watch. 'I'm on a tight schedule, I'm afraid.' Ester nodded.

She hadn't been surprised that he would be returning to work at the hospital once he had introduced her to his father. All medical staff seemed to work endless hours.

At the house Dr Bentley Senior presented as a grumpy old man. Ester reminded herself that he was in pain and frustrated by his immobile situation.

She saw it as a personal goal to win him over by her kindness and her willingness to learn.

The house was beautiful and the son gave her a tour. It had been his family home and where he had grown up. It was clear he was very fond of the place.

Upstairs there was a lovely bedroom with a proper bed for Ester and a little room off it which would be ideal for Polly although originally it was probably a dressing-room.

'I can get hold of a suitable bed for your daughter and furnish her with some toys from the old nursery,' he told her.

The old man was indeed generous. There would be a regular allowance and all board and lodging included.

Ester would be required to prepare, cook and serve breakfast, luncheon and dinner.

She would eat breakfast with him but he often had guests to join him for luncheon or his evening meal.

'Father eats out at his club on Tuesdays and Thursdays so you will have time to yourself after luncheon on those days.

'You will not be needed again until breakfast the following morning.'

'Am I only required to cook?' Ester asked in surprise.

'Father has a cleaner who has been with us for years. She comes in each morning.

'My father likes to read the newspapers in the morning and would appreciate it if you could be available to discuss current political events.

'There is a wireless so you can listen

to the news.'

'What about medical assistance?'

Ester had noticed that the elderly doctor had a walking-stick but, other than that, she wasn't sure of his physical state.

'I'm sure, when the weather allows, he would appreciate a walk in the garden. The fresh air and exercise would do him good.

'There is a swing for your daughter to play on.' He smiled. 'What Father really needs is decent, home-cooked food and stimulating conversation.

'The fact that you have shown an interest in medicine is a real bonus. I'm sure you'll hit it off.'

★   ★   ★

Ester had been impressed by the sleeping arrangements and delighted that the young doctor had suggested he furnish Polly's little adjoining room with a cot and toys.

The old man himself had not spoken a great deal. The challenge of winning him over appealed to Ester.

But the thing that had tipped the balance was the swing in the garden. It reminded her of her own childhood garden and she loved the thought of Polly being able to live here, even though she herself would be little more than a paid servant.

'Shall we give it a three-month trial and see how things get on?' the son suggested. 'How soon can you start?'

'Almost at once, actually, though my supervisor is not going to be pleased,' Ester admitted.

She was aware that by the end of the following week her rent would be due again and she paid in arrears.

If she gave her landlord notice now she could leave at the end of the month without having to pay another month's rent.

'That's excellent! So, welcome, Mrs Sharp. Shall I drop you off at the Emporium?'

'That's very kind of you,' Ester said, 'but there's no need. It's so close to here that I'll walk.'

As they opened the front door, however, the rain, which had been a light drizzle, became suddenly heavier and so Ester accepted a lift.

Adam was waiting at the door to the Emporium. He stepped out with an umbrella when he saw the motor car pull up outside.

'We were getting worried about you,' he whispered to her after she thanked the doctor and he hurried her inside.

'We guessed you must have gone to meet your new employer. Was everything as you'd hoped?'

Once she was seated with him and Aunt Maud, Ester was surprised how excited she was as she relayed her news.

It was the prospect of living in such a lovely house and being able to give Polly a little room of her own, complete with toys and a swing in the garden.

'Not only that, I can have Tuesday and Thursday afternoons and evenings off, too. We can come and visit, and maybe I can help you out here.'

'You will always be welcome here,' Adam and Aunt Maud said together.

A New Home

Polly was always very quiet in front of Dr Bentley Senior. When she and her mother were alone she would ask when she was going to see Auntie Maud.

'We'll go on Thursday afternoon,' Ester promised although the child, of course, had no concept of time and kept wanting to fetch her coat.

The old doctor was a difficult man; nothing seemed to please him.

He almost blamed her for the outbreak of war, for his immobility, for shortages in some foods, even for the rain!

By contrast his son, who called round often, was charming and helped improve the relationship between Ester and his father.

She was still hopeful that she could win over her elderly employer and make him smile again but, for now, she would be happy if only he didn't grunt or snap at her so much.

Each week on a Tuesday afternoon

and again on a Thursday they would go just around the corner to visit Aunt Maud and Adam Boniface at the Emporium.

Both Ester and Polly always had a skip in their step as they headed for the old shop full of interesting articles, each item telling a story.

Now and again Ester would see an old acquaintance in the street and would stop for a chat. Sometimes they would ask her to take something to the pawnshop on their behalf.

She was much more wary about doing this now, however, after having been accused of theft when Ann's husband had given her that golden locket.

The weeks seemed to fly by and Ester was surprised to realise she was soon approaching the end of the month's trial period.

Nothing had been said but Ester was expecting to be called in by both father and son and for them to discuss how they all felt things were going.

For her part, she realised that it was

early days but she was pleased that, at
least, Dr Bentley ate well.

He often asked for a second helping
lately if there was one to be had.

Missing Child!

On Thursday morning Ester had listened to the news bulletin on the wireless as usual. She was ready to discuss the matters of the day with Dr Bentley Senior once he'd had time to read the newspaper.

As she was busy preparing luncheon Polly sat in the kitchen playing with some wooden bricks. As always Bertie was by her side.

On this particular occasion the doctor was entertaining an old work colleague and so they were to dine upstairs in the dining-room.

Ester would have her lunch in the kitchen with Polly. Sometimes the daily help would stay for a bowl of soup with her but today she was in a tizz because her son was coming home from the war!

He only had a few hours before he would have to be back at the barracks, ready for heaven knew what.

'I won't be a moment, Polly,' Ester

told the child as she set a tray with food to take up to the dining-room for the doctor and his guest.

'We'll have lunch as soon as I come down. Will you go and wash your hands?'

Ester took the tray upstairs and was delighted when old Dr Bentley smiled at her appearance.

'Hmm, that smells delicious,' he said to her surprise.

She almost skipped back down the stairs to the kitchen, feeling happier than she had in quite a while.

It was good to know she had made the right decision. In many ways she felt blessed.

The arrangement of living-in whilst earning a little and being able to save, yet still being close to her dear friends Aunt Maud and Adam, was working out very well in Ester's opinion.

Back in the kitchen she picked up Polly's toys and put them back in the cardboard box. Then she called her for lunch.

Everywhere seemed eerily quiet and

Ester's heart began to pound.

Quickly she checked the boot room where she had left a chair for Polly to climb up on to wash her hands, giving her a little independence.

The towel was still neatly folded and there were no droplets of water on the floor.

It didn't look as though Polly had got around to washing her hands.

Ester put a dish over their luncheon and swiftly ran up the stairs to their rooms.

Again all was quiet and there was no sign Polly had been there.

'Polly?' she called, quietly at first, keeping her growing panic at bay.

Receiving no response her calls grew in volume, betraying her anxiety.

'Is something amiss?' Dr Bentley's guest popped his head round the corner of the dining-room door.

'My daughter, Polly, is missing. I can't find her anywhere!'

'Have you checked these rooms?' he asked, gesturing to a series of closed doors in the corridor.

Ester thought it highly unlikely that Polly would have entered any of them. She usually avoided these rooms because of old Dr Bentley's booming voice.

'I haven't, but . . .'

'Go and search again upstairs. I'll check here.'

Ester ran back up the stairs. She checked every room including Dr Bentley's bedroom. Then she remembered the nursery on the very top floor.

They had only been up there once but the room contained a rocking-horse to which Polly had taken a shine.

She checked the nursery, searched the bedrooms again and ran back downstairs, almost colliding with Dr Bentley's guest.

'No joy,' he told her. 'Might she be in the garden?'

He accompanied her down the stairs and out into the garden.

Just as they were going out, Ester noticed Polly's coat was missing. Even though it was winter Polly loved to run around in the garden.

She kept to the path that ran round the edge; it was out of sight of the large window where Dr Bentley often sat.

'Polly!'

There was no sign of the child. Ester and the guest returned to the warmth of the kitchen, only to notice the side gate was ajar.

Without bothering to fetch her own coat Ester ran out and scanned the length and breadth of the street. There was no sign of Polly.

Instinctively Ester hurried along the road in the direction of the Emporium.

She and Polly had made this journey several times and it would be familiar to the little girl.

Well Respected

Ester burst into the Emporium.

'Polly! Polly! Are you here?'

Adam appeared in his overcoat.

'I was about to go and tell you she's here. She arrived alone only a moment ago. Has something happened?'

Ester burst into tears of relief and joy.

'Come in,' Aunt Maud fussed and set about making tea to calm Ester down.

'Oh, no!' Ester cried. 'Doctor Bentley will want his dessert and I need to let them know I've found Polly.'

'Go,' Aunt Maud said. 'She's safe here. Don't be long; your tea will get cold.'

Ester hurried back, wiping away her tears fiercely. She was frozen by the time she slipped through the side gate and into the warm kitchen.

Hastily she wiped the mud from her shoes and smartened herself up before taking an apple pie and jug of thick cream to the two gentlemen upstairs in the dining-room.

'I found her,' she said without waiting to be asked. 'She made it to the Emporium.'

'The pawnbroker's?' the doctor asked.

'We're friends with Mr Boniface and his aunt,' Ester explained. 'They've been very good to us.'

'The Boniface family are well respected, been here for years,' the doctor agreed. I didn't realise his aunt was still alive.'

'I don't believe she's a true aunt but a good friend of the family.'

'I see.' Dr Bentley seemed to notice her muddy shoes and gave her a look.

Ester collected their dirty plates, served their pie and cream and retreated.

Her hands were shaking by the time she reached the kitchen and it was all she could do not to drop the tray.

She cleaned her shoes, wrapped up their lunch and placed it in her basket.

She rinsed the plates and was about to go upstairs, to clear the table and check whether they required anything else, when footsteps echoed on the back staircase and Mr Bentley's guest appeared.

'I'm glad you found her,' he said with grandfatherly affection, 'and that she's safe and sound. We're off to the club.

'Doctor Bentley says goodnight and that he'll have scrambled egg for breakfast.'

'Thank you.' Ester's hands were trembling with the shock of it all. 'Thank you so much for your help.'

A Proposition

Having completed her chores Ester returned to the Emporium. She wasn't sure what she was going to say to Polly.

She knew she had to make it clear that she was never to run off like that again, but it made her wonder why Polly had gone in the first place.

Polly was 'helping' Adam in the shop. They were polishing some brass buttons with an old rag.

'We've had a little chat,' Aunt Maud said softly as she made a fresh pot of tea. 'Polly doesn't like Doctor Bentley — he has a loud voice. Does he shout at her?'

'On the contrary, he's tried to engage her in conversation. She goes terribly shy and hides behind me. It's most unlike her.

'He is a little deaf and I suppose his voice is loud but I wouldn't say he shouted.'

'Is it working out for all of you?'

'Until today,' Ester replied, 'I thought

it was going very well!'

The shop door opened.

'Don't move,' Aunt Maud said.

Ester was grateful for the chance just to sit and sip the hot, sweet, black tea. She listened to Aunt Maud's quiet voice as she listened to the woman's story as to why she was pawning her pillowcases.

Having finished her tea Ester wandered into the shop. She watched Adam, his sleeves rolled up, and Polly, sitting beside him on a crate, as they polished up a tin of brass buttons.

Ester sighed. Polly was at home here. There were never cross voices; never any need to tiptoe about.

Polly always tiptoed in Dr Bentley's house, Ester realised. Did she live in fear of disturbing him or attracting his attention?

'You look full of worries,' Aunt Maud said once the woman had gone, leaving behind her pillowcases. 'Do you want to talk?'

'I just don't know what to do,' Ester admitted.

She bit back the tears that threatened. She didn't want Polly to see her cry.

Adam looked up and gave a little nod to his aunt.

'We've been having a talk,' she told Ester. 'Come and see what you think.'

She led Ester to the front of the shop. There were large bay windows on either side of the shop entrance.

'We're thinking of clearing this area and partitioning it off with a few screens. You could have a long table and a few chairs.

'Adam has put aside a dressmaker's dummy for you. You could have your own little shop here. Polly can 'work' beside you. When she's older we'll teach her to sew.'

The tears began to roll down Ester's cheeks. These people were so kind, so generous!

Aunt Maud went on.

'If you had a fitting I could take Polly into the lounge with me. Likewise, if we're busy, such as on a Wednesday afternoon, then you might give us a hand behind the counter.

'What do you say? Could we make it work?'

Adam had come to join them. Holding his hand was Polly. She held one shiny button in her other hand and held it out for inspection.

'You've done a very good job,' they all told her.

Aunt Maud reached for Polly and led her back to fetch the tin and collect the rags.

'Well, what do you think?' Adam asked.

Ester looked up at him. He looked taller and more handsome than ever.

His kindness broke her heart. What did she have to offer in return?

'You've mentioned having a sewing shop of your own,' he was saying. 'I know this set up is not ideal but you can have a window display.

'From time to time we acquire man-nequins; you could use them to display your outfits.'

'This is all so kind,' she told him ear-nestly. 'You know I would love to have a place for dressmaking and alterations and I do believe there is a market for it.

'I know that Polly would be happy here, too.'

'But?' He raised an eyebrow.

'Where would we live?'

She hated the thought of going back to the damp little room they used to rent.

'We've thought about that, too,' Adam replied. 'My aunt is concerned about her house being locked up and vacant.

'We thought you and Polly could share the upstairs apartment here — the room I'm currently using. I'll move to Aunt Maud's.'

'I couldn't put you out!' Ester began.

'I would be doing her a favour by occupying her house and you would be doing me a favour by being on hand for Aunt Maud.

'She needs a hand with some things, a woman's touch. This way we can all look after each other.

'It would be nice to have you and Polly back. We've missed you.'

Ester's heart did another flip, especially the way he smiled at her.

A second later she pulled herself together. This was a business arrangement.

'My month's trial is coming up,' she told him. 'I'll let Doctor Bentley know it's not working out.

'I don't think he'll be surprised; he tells me often enough that his housekeepers never stay more than a month.'

'That's excellent news,' Adam said, 'and I didn't even need to play my trump card!'

'What's that?' Ester felt quite light-headed all of a sudden.

'I thought you'd be disappointed that you wouldn't be able to continue with your medical training,' he began.

'Huh. Doctor Bentley made it quite plain what he thinks of female doctors. He was never going to impart any of his medical knowledge to me,' she interrupted.

'I was going to suggest that, one day a week, you could volunteer at the new hospital for wounded soldiers. They're looking for people like you.'

'Mummy go!' Polly piped up from behind them. 'I look after Bertie and Daddy.'

All Settled!

The following morning Ester tactfully mentioned that her month's trial had come to an end and that she felt it wasn't working out for any of them.

She expected the old man to agree with her but he grunted and sent her away.

His son arrived mid-morning, having been summoned by a message through the daily.

Ester was called to the study to face both doctors.

'What's the meaning of this?' the son asked. 'Have we not provided you with everything you need?'

'You've been most thoughtful, most generous,' she assured them.

'Yet you feel the need to find alternative employment. Why?' he demanded.

'I don't believe your father is satisfied with my work.' She took a deep breath. 'I think, too, Polly misses Aunt Maud, the lady who cared for her.'

'Surely she could continue to care for the child?' he said. 'That problem would be easily solved.'

'It's not that simple. Aunt Maud is in need of care herself now. If I live on the premises I can provide that.

'She's been very good to me and now I have a chance to pay her back.'

'We'll see about that!' the young doctor stormed out of the room.

'Is there any of that cake left?' old Dr Bentley asked. 'That would go down very well with a nice cup of tea.'

Ester disappeared back to the kitchen and began to prepare tea and cake for the doctor.

It saddened her that things had not worked out but she had missed using her precious sewing-machine and looked forward to using it again and to be able to design and make all sorts of outfits.

As she waited for the pot to boil she imagined what she would make first.

No sooner had she taken up tea and cake for old Dr Bentley than the door opened and the son was there, looking triumphant.

'It's all settled. I've spoken to Boniface and told him you're staying here.'

Ester couldn't imagine how the conversation had gone between the two men but she was determined to find out.

She served tea without saying a word. As soon as they went off to their club she wrapped Polly up in her coat and they ventured out, back to the Emporium.

Another Surprise

The doorbell gave its familiar chime, announcing their arrival. Aunt Maud appeared and beckoned them in.

Polly made herself at home while Ester followed Maud into the kitchen alcove.

'Has young Doctor Bentley been here?' she asked in a whisper.

Then she turned as she heard Adam give a discreet cough.

'Has he?'

'I sincerely hope that man has a better manner with his patients than he had with me earlier,' Adam told her. 'He didn't listen to a word I said; he just made his demands and left.

'There was no opportunity for discussion. I assume he believes he's got his own way?'

Ester nodded.

'He told me he'd spoken with you and that I was to remain in my job and not mention it again!'

All this time Ester had been expecting

Aunt Maud to begin making tea, as she always did.

Instead, she produced a couple of homemade gingerbread men and asked Polly to come and give her a hand with something special.

Ester wondered if something was amiss. The look Aunt Maud gave Adam on her way into the shop had been odd.

'Am I now back to square one?' Ester fretted. 'I wouldn't be too upset about it if only Polly was more settled. What can I do to . . .'

'Hush,' Adam said quietly as he pushed closed the door. 'Take it as a compliment that the Bentleys value you and want you to remain in their employ.

'If you had a choice, Ester, where would you choose to be?'

'Here, of course. Although I do feel bad about driving you out of your room!'

'We've already discussed that and you're not,' Adam told her firmly.

He was acting rather strangely, she

thought. He was moving from side to side and twisting his fingers awkwardly, as though he was about to deliver bad news.

'Is everything all right?' she asked. 'What is it?'

'Aunt Maud and I have come up with a plan,' he said at last.

Ester nodded.

'She already mentioned the dress-maker's 'shop' in the corner.'

She had noticed with delight that someone had already installed two painted screens to define the area.

A dressmaker's dummy had also appeared from nowhere and stood waiting.

Adam then did the most extraordinary thing. He went down on one knee and reached out for her hand!

'Ester Sharp, will you marry me?' he asked throatily.

Ester gasped.

'You just need to agree,' he went on, 'and I'll go immediately to see Doctor Bentley. I'll explain that, as my wife, you cannot possibly continue as his house-keeper.'

'You would do that for me?' She was astounded.

'No, Ester, I'm not doing it just for you.' Adam smiled. 'I'm doing it for me. Because I think I fell in love with you the very first time you came in my shop.

'You were like a breath of fresh air and I've not been able to think of anything else since.

'I've grown to love you and Polly even more now we've had a chance to get to know each other.

'Do you think, given time, you might ever love me, too?'

'Oh, Adam, I do love you! You've always treated me with such kindness and generosity and you're so patient and good with Polly.

'But marriage is a huge commitment, you know. You have to be absolutely sure that you're not just wishing to be the hero and rescue me once again.'

'You are right,' Adam replied. 'Marriage is a big undertaking. More so in our situation because we have a ready-made family with your Polly and Aunt Maud.'

He squeezed her hand.

'One day we might give Polly a brother or sister, too. Is that also your wish?'

Ester nodded, her eyes brimming.

Adam took her in his arms and his lips sought hers. They were as warm and gentle as she'd hoped.

'I would have proposed on the night of the Picture Palace, you looked so beautiful in that green dress. But I'm afraid I lost my nerve.

'It was my aunt who encouraged me. She would like us all to live in her house, if you'd be willing?'

'Yes! Perhaps we could convert her front parlour into a bedroom for her so she doesn't have to bother with the stairs,' Ester mused. 'Do you think she'd be happy with that?'

'She will be thrilled to bits!' Adam promised. 'Come on, let's find Polly and Aunt Maud, then I'll go and explain the situation to the Bentley's. Their loss is my gain.'

He reached out his hand for Ester's and together they went to share the good news to the rest of their ready-made family.

We do hope that you have enjoyed reading this large print book.

Did you know that all of our titles are available for purchase?

We publish a wide range of high quality large print books including:
Romances, Mysteries, Classics
General Fiction
Non Fiction and Westerns

Special interest titles available in large print are:
The Little Oxford Dictionary
Music Book, Song Book
Hymn Book, Service Book

Also available from us courtesy of Oxford University Press:
Young Readers' Dictionary
(large print edition)
Young Readers' Thesaurus
(large print edition)

For further information or a free brochure, please contact us at:
Ulverscroft Large Print Books Ltd.,
The Green, Bradgate Road, Anstey,
Leicester, LE7 7FU, England.
Tel: (00 44) **0116 236 4325**
Fax: (00 44) **0116 234 0205**

Other titles in the
Linford Romance Library:

STRANGERS AT FURZE POINT

Teresa Ashby

The wedding of Noah Walsh and Beth Clarke at Laburnum Villa is a time for love and celebration. But a chance meeting at the reception throws Fergus Thompson's life into disarray, and puts vet Anna Novak in a spin. Meanwhile, the appearance of a man from Rosita Tennyson's past makes her consider turning her back on the town she loves . . .

THE COWBOY'S TREASURE

Jill Barry

Katie is a young governess who leaves Yorkshire to take over her aunt's teaching post at a small country town school in America. Not long after she arrives, she meets Ben, a young cattleman who is also new in town. On riding in, Ben had happened upon an old man who had been attacked. Although unable to keep the stranger alive, he learned a secret from him: one linked to Katie's aunt . . .

DOLPHIN'S KISS

Dawn Knox

Growing up in Sydney in the early 1800s, Abigail Moran knows only the constraints of a privileged life, and that she must hide the birthmark on her left hand at all costs. Yet the mark might prove to be the key that unlocks the secrets of her turbulent start in life aboard a convict ship — and, on a very different boat trip, it could open her eyes to real love . . .